RAIDERS NIGHT

RAIDERS NIGHT

Robert Lipsyte

HarperTempest

An Imprint of HarperCollins*Publishers*

Library of Congress Cataloging-in-Publication Data

Lipsyte, Robert.

Raiders night / Robert Lipsyte.—1st ed.

p.   cm.

Summary: Matt Rydeck, co-captain of his high school football team, endures a traumatic season as he witnesses a vicious assault on a rookie player by teammates and grapples with his own use of performance-enhancing drugs.

ISBN-10: 0-06-059946-4 (trade bdg.) — ISBN-13: 978-0-06-059946-1 (trade bdg.)

ISBN-10: 0-06-059947-2 (lib. bdg.) — ISBN-13: 978-0-06-059947-8 (lib. bdg.)

[1. Football—Fiction. 2. Steroids—Fiction. 3. Drug abuse—Fiction. 4. Rape—Fiction.] I. Title.

PZ7.L67Rai 2006

[Fic]—dc22   2005017865

CIP

AC

Typography by R. Hult

1 2 3 4 5 6 7 8 9 10

❖

First Edition

For the team—
*Kyle, Jessie,
Sam, Alfred, Mimi,
and Lois*

ONE

The Back Pack hit the gym in the early afternoon, Matt in the lead, before the yuppies marched in from work, while the young moms were rushing out to pick up their kids from day camp. Matt liked the way their hot eyes roamed over him, wondered if they knew he was still in high school, wondered if they cared. He felt big and hard. Excited. Was it the moms or what was waiting for him upstairs, the iron weights that would make him even bigger, harder. And the juice.

Brody poked him from behind with the football he always carried. "Check the headlights on the one in blue."

"Someday I'm gonna stick that ball up your ass."

"Ooooh, don't tease me, big boy."

Matt led them through the downstairs crowd of designer spandex and pastel sweats, cuties perched on shiny machines jiggling away to love songs as they pretended to work out. What did they know about working out? He liked the sense of leaving their soft world behind as he led the Back Pack up the metal steps into the stink and clang of the second floor, the real workout room.

He was glad they had beaten the linemen to the gym today. Give us a chance to get our session going without Ramp's crap.

The ironheads were there; they were always there, older white guys screaming each other into one more pec-busting rep. They wore tank tops and bandannas that looked like they were soaked in diesel fuel. One of them called out a singsong, half-mocking "Rai-derz."

Tyrell raised two fists. "Raiders rule, niggaz!"

The ironheads liked that and banged metal plates. Some of them had gone to Nearmont High and played ball.

"Matt?" The gym owner, Monty, came out of his office and beckoned him over. "New shipment's in."

Matt nodded and felt the excitement rise. Perfect timing. Load up just before camp so the juice kicks in during the two-a-days when we really need it. He flashed the Back Pack a thumbs-up. Hope they all brought their wallets.

They dressed quickly. They were jittery, psyched for the last heavy workout before camp. Tyrell, as usual, complained about the music on the upstairs speakers, a pounding mix of disco and heavy metal. The ironheads

2

controlled those CDs. For now. See what happens if we win Conference this year.

Matt caught Pete sneaking peeks at himself in the mirror. Pete was more self-conscious than the rest of them about the pimples on his shoulders. Backne they called it. From the steroids. Price you pay. Pete's girlfriend, Lisa, wasn't so sure it was worth the price. She'd said as much, and Pete listened to her. Girls hear about the side effects, but how could they know the feeling of watching a muscle grow bigger and harder? Pete flexed his biceps when he thought no one was looking, as if to remind himself that Lisa didn't know everything.

Matt said, "Quads and glutes win games." He wondered if he was taking this captain thing too seriously.

"Tyrell says bicep curls win hot girls," said Tyrell. He mimicked Pete's flex.

Pete, embarrassed, snapped his shirt at Tyrell, who laughed and danced just out of range. They loved to watch Tyrell move. He had radar. He glided like a phantom. He was the best running back in the conference. If we stay healthy and tight, Matt thought, this could be our season. Maybe State. Senior year, what a way to go.

Out on the mats, stretching, Matt could tell Brody's mind was heading to the same place.

"We got a shot." Brody's big freckly face had that dreamy look. Probably imagining himself winning the state title. With a quarterback sneak. Not a forty-yard bomb to me or a handoff to Tyrell, but a heroic scramble out of a collapsing pocket and a desperate lunge over the goal line. Behind his back, some of the guys called him All-Brody. Dad thought he didn't throw to Matt enough. But Brody was all right. Best friend on the team.

"One day at a time," said Matt.

"You're, like, channeling Coach Mac," said Brody.

"You ready to put the bar where your mouth is?" Matt held up the clipboard with their workout schedule.

"See what I mean?"

They started with squats, lunges, and power cleans to build up their legs and lower backs for the explosive starts off the line of scrimmage. These were the most intense exercises in the daily program the coaches had laid out in the spring. Matt had come to realize that if they left those exercises to the end of the session, they would slack off, especially Pete and Brody. They preferred to work harder on the lat pull downs, the curls and flys to build up their upper bodies for the beach. But they listened to Matt. He was their leader. Tyrell had named them the Back Pack, the four starting backfield seniors. Brody, Pete, and Matt had played together since PeeWee. Tyrell had joined them as a sophomore after he came out from New York, staying at his aunt's house during the week so he could go to Nearmont High.

The linemen stomped in, Ramp bellowing, "Yo, Rydek, your girls done yet?"

Before Matt could respond, Tyrell shouted, "Where you been? Stop off for lunch at the hog farm?"

Ramp cursed, raised a finger, and led the linemen into the locker room.

Matt waited until they were out of earshot. "Chill."

"Nobody cool says chill no more."

"Our last season, last chance to win Conference." He glared at Tyrell until he nodded and started pulling dumbbells off the rack. "Let's be a team."

"You always right, Cap'n Matt, sir."

Matt and Brody moved to the benches. It took a few reps to clear his head, but once Matt felt the blood pumping again, all the good feelings came back. He concentrated on visualizing his muscles swell and harden as he lay on the bench and pushed the bar up toward Brody's face. Familiar, comforting pains flooded his chest and shoulders as he fought his arms straight under 275 pounds.

"Up, c'mon, up, you pussy," growled Brody, spotting him. "You can do it."

Matt yelled as his elbows locked. Personal best.

"Good job," shouted Brody. "It's all you, man."

"Nice start," snickered Ramp, his big potato head looming above Matt. "Now put some weight on the bar." He swaggered off. The linemen would be lifting at least fifty pounds more.

They worked out for two hours, tapering on the

rowing machines, cooling down on the treadmill. They watched Ramp and the linemen scream their way through fifty-pound flys while the ironheads nodded.

In the shower room, they checked each other out. You never look so good as after a heavy workout, thought Matt. Everything looks bigger. Tyrell's shoulders were black bowling balls, his butt was stone. Imagine if he juiced with us. Tyrell said he was afraid of losing quickness. They'd argued over that. Olympic sprinters used steroids and growth hormone all the time. But Tyrell said they just blew ahead straight while he needed to cut and fade. Matt thought it might be about money. Tyrell never had much. In the city, Tyrell lived with his grandmother in a housing project.

Tyrell split when they headed for Monty's office behind the one-way glass mirrors. You couldn't see in but Monty could see out. He opened the door before Matt knocked.

"You're gonna love this stuff," Monty said as they filed in. He closed the door. "I got a new supplier, Canadian. He puts together stacks for NFL players."

"How much?" asked Brody.

"For you guys, I'm sticking with the old prices. This batch is $220."

Monty took a FedEx box out of a metal locker and began unpacking bottles. He spread a clean white towel across the top of his desk and laid out the bottles, syringes, needles, and alcohol swabs. Monty was in his forties, but he still had the shape of a bodybuilder even if the muscles had shrunk and softened. As usual, Matt was fascinated by his precision. Monty stripped the paper wrappers off the syringes, screwed on the needles, and pulled off their plastic guards with his teeth. He stabbed a needle through the rubber top of a bottle and slowly drew out the oily yellow liquid.

Pete groaned softly. He was solid and dependable on the field, but he always started sweating and swaying about now. Still, he hadn't fainted in more than a year.

Monty flicked a forefinger against a syringe and pushed a drop of liquid through the tip of the needle. "Who's first?"

"Matt's number one in my book," said Pete, raising a middle finger. He was white as a ghost but trying to keep it together.

"Grab your ankles, Matt." Monty always said that.

Matt loosed the drawstring on his shorts and let them drop to his flip-flops. No underwear in this weather. He bent over the desk. Monty slapped him high on the buttock to numb the skin and rubbed it with alcohol. Matt felt a pinch and a sting as he drove in the needle, then the sensation of something cold sliding into the big muscle.

"This is the Decadurabolin," said Monty. "Stacked with testosterone. Gonna rip you big-time, man. It's the all-pro cocktail. I'll give you some Danabol pills, too."

Monty slipped out the needle and pressed the swab on the puncture site. Matt imagined the steroids rushing through his system, finding the muscles, healing them, building them, making them stronger.

Brody pushed Pete forward. He was shivering as he gripped the edge of the desk. Pete closed his eyes as Monty drilled him. The weekly injections turned Pete to jelly, even though his big, soft backside swallowed the needle. Brody didn't seem to notice the shot.

Watching them, Matt felt a surge of brotherhood. He felt even closer to them in here than in the weight room or on the field. Taking the shots proved their commitment to the team and to each other. We'll do whatever it takes to get bigger, get better, to win.

There was a knock at the door, then Ramp's voice. "Yo, Doctor Monty. Ready for the men?"

"Just a minute." Monty grinned at Matt. "No excuses now. Gonna kick some this season, right?"

"Right," said Matt. This is our time, he thought.

TWO

The softball game had started by the time they got to the town field. The lights were on. From the parking lot, Matt could hear his father barking, "Let's get a hit, get a hit, no pitcher, no pitcher." Brody flipped Matt the football as they walked but didn't say anything. Brody's dad was a piece of work, too. They didn't need to talk about it. Matt rubbed the football between his palms before he flipped it back. The pebbly skin reminded him he was a football player, even here on Dad's turf. Brody had started carrying the ball everywhere two summers ago, after he went to a quarterback camp where an NFL coach told them that the great ones even slept with the ball. It was all about making the ball an extension of their bodies. The Back Pack joked about Brody shagging pigskin, but they understood. Wherever you were, the ball brought you back to who you were.

9

They took their time strolling to the stands, tossing the ball, letting the crowd catch sight of them. People waved. A few little boys ran up just to follow them like puppies. The boldest one tugged at their baggy shorts and held out his hands for the ball. Matt asked him, "What inning?"

"Second. No score, Matt." The kid sounded proud to say his name.

Matt felt good. Warm and hard and big. He avoided looking at his father, coaching at third base.

"Matt, Mattie, Matt, over here." His brother, Junie, large and loud, was bouncing on the grandstand, waving him over. Matt waved back and signaled him to sit down, be quiet. Too late. Dad had spotted Matt. He felt the where-you-been glare before he saw it. Dad wanted the whole family at his games. Mom would be up in the stands somewhere with her friends.

Brody asked, "You going to Lexie's?"

"You?"

Brody shrugged. "Might as well. Last party before hell."

"Pick me up after the game?"

"I'm driving?"

"Your turn," said Matt.

"What about Pete?"

"Who knows? Might have to paint Lisa's toenails tonight."

Brody laughed. "Okay."

"See you after. Gotta go sit with Junie."

"Gotta conduct a chassis inspection." Brody pointed the football toward a bursting red tank top. "Catch you later."

It took Matt a few minutes to work his way into the stands. Men wanted to say hello, ask about the coming season. Old ladies clucked over his sleeveless Baybodies T-shirt. He'd picked it up on a recruiting trip to Michigan State when he'd gotten wasted at a strip club with some of the college players. Dad hated the shirt, which was why he was wearing it.

He knew only a few girls in the stands, mostly the younger sisters of friends and the twenty-something girl-friends of players on Dad's softball team. Most of the better senior girls were still off on vacation or in college prep camps or getting ready for tonight's party. Mandy wouldn't be home from cheerleader camp until after he left for training camp. She'd been gone for almost two weeks. He rarely thought about her when she wasn't around. He'd started leaving his cell off when he thought she might call. Time enough to figure all that out after camp.

"Matt?" A short, bug-eyed kid he dimly recognized from school was hopping alongside. Looked like a frog. "Matt, I write for the *Nearmont Eye*, and . . ."

"The school paper?"

"No, we're the alternate, online, totally independent."

He puffed up, just like a frog. "I'd like to interview you about the coming season, not the usual stuff, but the real—"

"After we're back from camp, okay? I got to see my brother now." He didn't wait for a response.

Junie wrapped an arm around his neck when he sat down. "What's up, CyberPup?"

It was a line from Junie's favorite cartoon show. Matt groaned. "I'm in your power." Junie's arm was big but flabby. Got to get him into a fitness routine. Dad said he would but never did. Can't blame him for that—he's working all the time.

"Where you hiding the microchips?" said Junie.

"Right here with the potato chips." Matt grabbed a handful of Junie's belly through his blue Rydek Gourmet Catering T-shirt. Junie giggled and released his grip.

"Where you been, Matty?"

"At the gym." No need to tell him we stopped for burgers.

"Dad's been looking for you."

"Here I am." He tried to keep the annoyance out of his voice. Only make Junie nervous. "Let's watch the game."

Dad was stomping around the third-base coaching box, hands on hips, chest out, spitting sunflower seeds. Freddy Heinz, Brody's older brother, dug into the batter's box. Freddy had held all of Nearmont High's passing records until Brody started breaking them. Freddy had torn up his shoulder in a bar fight his sophomore year at Iowa State and switched to defensive back, then lost his scholarship and come home. He did landscaping now and drove a truck for Rydek Gourmet Catering. Dad had built a powerhouse softball team out of old Nearmont jocks who'd come back home and needed jobs after busting in college or pro ball, like he did.

"Let's do it, Freddy." Dad was clapping and shouting. "Go yard, go yard."

"What's *goyar*?" asked Junie.

"Go yard," said Matt. "Means go deep, hit a homer."

"Oh." Junie hated to feel dumb.

Matt squeezed the back of his neck. "Some TV guy made it up. I didn't know it, either."

"You didn't?" Junie perked up. "Go yard, Freddy."

Two on, two out, and Freddy grounded to short to end the inning. Dad shook his head and gave him the why-can't-you-do-what-I-tell-you-to-do glare. Know that one, too, thought Matt. The softball team had a shot at the league title this year, and Dad had been calling extra practices. Brody said his brother was complaining, but when you worked for the guy, you had to show up.

I work for the guy and I have to show up for my football games and his softball games, Matt thought. That's my work. Matt made a mental note to send Dad an e-mail invoice for catering work he hadn't done. Dad would put more money on Matt's debit card so he could pay Monty. They never talked about the steroids, although Matt knew that Dad talked to Monty. The Vicodin was easier because the orthopedic surgeon who treated Matt for back pain was pretty free with prescriptions and Dad paid the drugstore bill directly. Dad and the doctor both had to know how much Matt was taking, and they didn't care as long as he scored touchdowns. He swallowed down the anger that bubbled up in his throat. Chill, Matt, tomorrow you're out of here.

Rydek Catering took the field and Dad swaggered out to the mound. He was Monty's age and still pitching. They'd gone to Nearmont High together, both got football scholarships, but Dad skipped college to sign with the Mets for a small bonus. He spent two seasons in the minors but never got the chance to find out if he was good enough to make it to the Show. When he was twenty, his dad died of a heart attack and he had to come home and take over the family's small catering business, which he hated. He was married by then, and Junie was born. Years and years of doctor's bills there. He'd built up the business over time, but he was still pissed off at missing his chance.

"Mom wants you." Junie poked him and pointed to the top of the stands.

When Matt found Mom, she was mouthing the word, "Dinner?"

Matt shook his head and mouthed, "Party."

She rolled her eyes and turned to say something to Brody's mom, who smiled and waved at Matt. In the right clothes, from a distance, Brody's mom could pass for a high school girl. The guys agreed she was the hottest mom. He felt a warm splash run down from his chest. Feeling horny with Mandy away. The juice does it, too.

Dad's barking voice brought him back to the game. Chest first, he was marching toward the plate umpire, who had just called a fourth ball.

"Dad's really mad," said Junie. He sounded upset. He'd never gotten used to Dad's screaming.

"He's not so mad," said Matt. "It's just part of the game. He'll pretend he's angry so he gets his way." When Junie kept staring at him, he said, "He'll get over it before he comes home. Dad yells at the umpire so next time the umpire will be afraid to call a ball and he'll call a strike instead."

It took Junie a moment to digest it, then he smiled. "You know everything, Matt."

"Right about that, Ace." He punched his brother lightly, glad to make him smile, sad that Junie was seven years older.

The game dragged on. The score was tied. Swarms of bugs attracted by the lights dive-bombed spectators and players. Only Dad refused to slap them away, to acknowledge they even existed. Tough guy. Matt felt the old mix of admiration and anger. Dad teaching him to box by trading punches with him, always hitting back a little harder than Matt hit him. How many times had he heard Dad say, "Don't cry," and later, "Don't rub," and always, "Don't ever let them know you're hurting." Dad never showed pain, even when Matt started landing hard shots. Be good to get out of the house for five days.

In the seventh, Dad clubbed a looping fly into left-center and lumbered to first. Anybody else on the team would have gotten to second, maybe even third, but Dad stood proudly on the base, grinning for a moment before he finally signaled for a pinch runner. He really did want to win this game, thought Matt.

Back in the coaching box, he started screaming at the pitcher, trying to crack his concentration. But the pitcher was an older guy who ignored him. Wish I could do that, thought Matt.

Two outs, then Freddy Heinz was up again, working the count. He checked his swing on a pitch that Matt thought nicked the inside corner for a third strike to end the game, but the umpire called it a ball. The pitcher lost his cool and started yelling. The ump turned his back. Dad grinned at the crowd. Maybe he had intimidated him after all. It had worked before.

Freddy lined the next pitch deep into right field. The pinch runner scored to win the game. Junie was jumping and shouting, "We won, we won." He knew the old man would be in a good mood. Ice cream tonight.

Matt and Junie went out on the field. Mom joined them for a group hug. Dad swaggered over, grinning, kissing Mom, ruffling Junie's hair. Matt stuck out his hand to Dad, who grabbed it and pulled him into a half hug, squeezing him. He whispered in his ear, "Got to rattle those pussy umps, what I tell you?"

"You told me." Easy way out, and it left a sour taste in his mouth. He always felt smaller around Dad, even now that he was taller than him.

Just want to get through this year and out of town, and away from him. Matt's chest and shoulders were aching from the workout. Some beer and Vicodin would fix that. Then the last party before hell.

He was looking forward to hell. It was out of town.

THREE

Matt floated into the party a step behind Brody, who opened holes in the crowd with his smile. Brody reached out for guys to tap fists and girls to feel up. Ever since he was in PeeWee, All-Brody had acted like he was walking on a red carpet, but nobody ever seemed to mind. He could say anything to anybody. Guys trusted him in the huddle and girls couldn't keep their hands off him. He had left the football in the car. He was looking to score tonight.

The beer and Vic buzz carried Matt over the upturned faces. "Yo, Matt . . . Lookin' good, my man. . . . Where's Amanda? . . . Ready for hell, hoss?" He felt the words more than heard them, like hundreds of fingers plucking at him. Good thing Brody's driving tonight. Matt grinned back at people, winked, tapped a few fists, squeezed a few soft arms that came out of the crowd to encircle him like snakes and then fell away, brushing the length of his body. He smelled perfume and armpits. He waved back at Pete, in a corner with Lisa. They talked about everything. Pathetic, Matt thought, then wondered what it would be like to have someone you could really talk to.

"Start the party," Ramp bellowed. "Captains are here." His shoulders cleared a path and he was suddenly beside Matt, throwing a heavy arm around his neck, thrusting a can of beer in his hand. In this kind of crowd, Ramp always acted like they were buds. Otherwise, he made wiseass remarks and kept his distance. Been like that since PeeWee, teammates but never friends.

"Wassup?" Can't just blow Ramp off with everybody watching.

"Hear about the transfer from Bergen Central?" said Ramp.

Bergen Central was in another conference. He didn't know any of their players. "What about?"

"Sophomore tight end. Thinks he's just gonna show up and play." Ramp sounded angry. Ramp was a great linebacker, but only a so-so tight end. He didn't want any competition.

"He'll back you up," said Matt.

"We'll see what he's got." Ramp tightened his arm around Matt's neck. Matt thought of Dad squeezing him. "Where's Mandy?"

"Cheerleader camp." He considered ramming an elbow into Ramp's gut to loosen the grip. He was a little soft there. But it would take more energy than Matt had right now.

Ramp put his face close to Matt's ear. "Dog's night out? Find some strange meat, huh, woof, woof."

"Hey, is this like a same-sex thing?" Lexie glided up and made a big show of trying to separate them with her long bare arms. Matt could see most of her new breasts under her loose top.

"It's a three-way," said Ramp. He let go of Matt and made a grab for her but came up empty. She was quick. "Don't you want a test feel?"

She ignored him. "When's Amanda back?"

Matt's mind dragged, like a computer hard drive about to freeze. "Tomorrow?"

"Two of you come by?"

"Training camp."

Lexie tossed her blond hair. "So you boys can really get it on?" She cackled and danced away.

"Bitch needs more than new tits," said Ramp. "Who's she doing?"

Matt shrugged. He didn't keep up with that. Mandy's department.

"She needs a taste of the Ramp." He started after her. "Be a good dog."

Try to avoid him tonight, Matt thought, be enough of

him in camp. Ramp was a good captain for keeping the troops in line, but he couldn't leave his mean streak on the field. He scared girls, hardly ever scored if they weren't drunk. Matt wondered if it was just the beer fogging his windshield, or if the pain pills were kicking, too.

He settled into the fog, let it wrap him in a soft bumper. With Ramp gone, more guys came up to shake his hand, girls to rub against him. He didn't have to say much, just smile, nod. Hard to hear anyway, the music was amped so high. Mandy loved these parties. She was the queen. Have to be cool. Her spies were everywhere.

He spotted Lexie coming toward him, trying to shake off Ramp. Better run a route. He sidestepped around a couch and into another room. A guy who resembled him stared at him blankly. It took a beat to realize he was looking in a mirror. Someone offered the guy in the mirror a beer. He held up the one he had.

He followed a whiff of pot toward the back of the house, then out onto a deck. Tyrell was preaching to the stoners.

"Cap'n Matt?" Tyrell held out his blunt.

All I need, thought Matt, on top of the beer and pain pills. But he didn't want to wimp.

While Matt toked, Tyrell said, "Tyrell calls this man the Fre-quent Fly-er because he is the franchise, the stud. Matt Rydek could catch a hummingbird in a hurricane. His hands are softer than a baby's bee-hind."

A girl said, "You are a poet, Tyrell."

"Not Tyrell's only gift, juicy lady." He took the blunt from Matt and moved toward her.

A voice behind Matt, almost in his ear, said, "Your hands are softer than a baby's bee-hind?"

Matt turned, almost bumping a tall girl, short dark hair, full lips, big breasts. He dimly remembered her from last year.

"So, what do you use to keep your hands so soft?" She had a low voice.

"It's a football expression."

"Shut up." She had a tinkly laugh. Nice.

"Really." He wanted to explain that it just meant he could catch anything he could get his hands on, that footballs didn't bounce out of his grasp. But the words were stuck deep in his hard drive.

"You okay?" It sounded like a real question.

"Headache," he said. That was true.

"I've got something in my car that—"

"Thanks, I've had enough—"

"Ibuprofen." She laughed again and put a warm hand on his. "I'm maxed, too."

He angled for a better view of her. She had big eyes, nice teeth.

His cell vibrated. Be Mandy, he thought, checking up on me. Better answer. Get it over with quick. He mumbled something and turned his back on the girl. He flipped open the phone. "Eighty." It was his jersey number, a code with Mandy.

"This sucks." It was Brody.

"I'll stay for a while."

"Need a ride?"

"Got one." And some ibuprofen, too.

"Tomorrow." Brody hung up.

When he turned back, she was gone.

He tried to remember her name. Had he ever known it? He tried to bring up her face, but all he got were lips and eyes. Now I need a ride. He punched #1 on his speed dial but got Brody's voice mail. Maybe he's still here. He started toward the door. He felt as though he were walking in waist-high warm water, dense and salty. Ocean. Man, I am hammered. But the headache was okay, cottony, blotting out any other thoughts.

Lexie was in the middle of the living room, crying. Girls fluttered around her, cooing, patting her. One of them turned to glare at him. Terri. The one Mandy replaced. Get over it already. Like Coach says, Get past the past.

"Score yet?" Ramp dropped a meat hook on his shoulder.

Lexie was wailing now.

"What's her problem?" It was the kicker, Patel.

"Drama queen," said Ramp. "She bought new boobs to get attention and now she got it."

23

"Needs a pounding," said Patel. He was okay, but he was the only Indian on the team and tried too hard to sound like the other guys.

"I need a beer," said Ramp.

Patel scurried off. I need to get away from all this, thought Matt. Get out of the house, walk home if I have to. He shrugged off Ramp's arm and made his way across the room. But he had lost the sense of where he was. Lexie's dad was a contractor and the house was huge, a maze. Matt passed kids making out and then thought he passed them again.

Patel popped up and pressed a cold can into his hand. "Got you one, too, Matt."

"Thanks." It felt good rolled across his forehead.

It took forever to find the door. It was cooler outside. Did he really want to walk? Try Brody again.

"Ready?" The tall girl with the full lips came out of the shadows.

"Thought you left."

"I was waiting for you." Her hand on his arm guided him across the lawn.

Her car was on the road, a gray Jetta. She opened the passenger door for him. He strained to see her face. What was her name?

She started the engine, then reached across him to open the glove compartment. Her body was warm and soft on his lap. She rattled a little plastic bottle. "Take two." She put the pills in his hand. When he hesitated, she said, "Ibuprofen, remember?"

He washed them down with a gulp of warm beer. His forehead had cooked the can. He turned to thank her but her lips were in the way.

"I have soft hands, too," she said.

FOUR

He was lost again in the maze of dark streets, voices murmuring at him from behind garbage cans and parked cars. He thought about putting up the convertible's top as protection, but the windshield was filthy and he needed to be able to peer over it to see where he was going. But he couldn't see anyway. A car wash. He needed to get to a car wash. Hands began rapping on the metal skin of the car, a drumbeat, laughter. He recognized voices but couldn't remember the names. His cell phone vibrated but he couldn't find it. He knew it was the call he was waiting for. He drove faster until the car wash appeared, then drove right onto the tracks. The machinery rumbled and moved the car into the spray. He couldn't get the top up. Huge wet rags from the ceiling were slapping his face, crushing his chest. He couldn't breathe. He was drowning.

"Romo." Junie was trying to drag the big dog off him,

but she didn't want to stop licking Matt's face.

He sat up fast. Romo stepped backward onto his groin. "Romo!" Scared, she jumped off the bed. Junie followed to comfort her.

Dad stuck his head into the room. "Breakfast, let's go."

"Get outa here." Matt forced his eyes to focus on the clock. "It's eight twenty."

"Time to get up."

"Saturday."

"I'm going to be gone all day—"

"So what?" He was waking up and his head hurt.

"—and I want to talk to you before you leave for camp."

"What about?"

Dad took one long step into the room and reached for Matt's sheet. Romo howled. He had stepped on her tail. "Why is that dumb dog always in my way?"

"Not dumb," said Junie. He hugged her.

"Okay," said Matt quickly. He knew where this could go. "Be right down."

Dad stomped out of the room and down the stairs. Junie looked up at Matt. He and Romo both had hurt looks in their eyes.

"He didn't mean it," said Matt. Sure he did. "Go on down—be right there."

He closed his eyes, waiting for his head to quit

threatening to roll off his neck. He had gotten home very late, after the sky had started to lighten. They had driven around, talking. The girl was a talker, although he couldn't remember what they had talked about. They had stopped to get some food, then parked somewhere. She had soft hands all right, and a soft mouth. He couldn't remember her name.

He opened his eyes and got up slowly. The room shifted, the ceiling tilting down, the floor slanting up. Jerry Rice smiled at him from the big poster on the wall. No. 80, the greatest wide receiver of all time. Been wearing his number since middle school. Jerry must have been hungover a few mornings. Maybe not, the shape he stayed in for so long.

In big print over his signature, it read:

> *The biggest enemy of best is good.*
> *If you're satisfied with what's good,*
> *you'll never be the best.*

By the time Matt got downstairs, Dad was at the kitchen table shoveling in waffles and glaring at Junie and Romo. Mom had on her bright and perky TV-Mom look. Dad must really be pissed. "Waffles or eggs, Matt?"

"Just a shake." He wasn't hungry. "And some coffee?"

"Scrambled eggs," said Junie.

"Waffles," said Dad. "They're mixed already."

"It's no trouble," said Mom. She gave Dad a tight smile.

"This isn't a diner," he said. He turned to Matt. "I'm thinking of doing a meal at camp."

"What for?" That woke Matt up.

"The boys like a break from camp chow. Remember the barbecue?"

Two years ago. He was a sophomore. It was harder to stand up to Dad then, keep him out of his space. "Do it when we come back."

"Too many other people around, it's not a team thing."

"You're not on the team." That came out before he thought about it.

"Waffles coming up," chirped Mom.

Dad's face had lost expression, tightening into the bland mask he wore when he was getting angry. Eyes got cold. "I want to do the meal after the boys get settled. But before Raider Pride Night."

"How come?"

"That night can get hairy." Dad grinned. "You know which night that is?"

Last night of camp, everybody knows that, jerkoff. "Dunno."

"Big-shot captain doesn't know?"

"Ask Coach."

"Ramp probably knows."

"Ask him." He felt the anger rise.

"You got a real 'tude this morning."

"It's too early."

"Only if you're up all night."

Mom said, "Larry, it wasn't a school night."

"It was a football night," said Dad.

"A softball night," said Junie as he patted Romo. She was whimpering.

"Can't you shut that dog up? Bad enough she's dumb, she's a pussy. World's fraidiest rottweiler."

"She's not even half rottweiler," said Mom.

"Well, that explains it," said Dad.

Matt measured the distance across the kitchen table as if Dad were a tackler who needed to be avoided or leveled. He must know he can't take me anymore, thought Matt. That's why we don't box anymore. Maybe it's time for some hard proof.

Chill. In a few hours you'll be on a bus out of here.

"When we come back," said Matt. "A barbecue when we come back."

"Can I go?" asked Junie. "I'll help. Do burgers." He mimed slapping meat patties on a grill.

"Wouldn't that be nice," said Mom.

"Can you drop Matt off at the bus?" Dad was changing the subject. Might have won that one. "I've got a bar mitzvah all the way up in Bergen Lakes."

"I'm covered," said Matt. All I need, Mom drops me off.

"No problem," said Mom.

"I'll drive myself," said Matt.

"Not likely," said Dad in his John Wayne voice. "Leave the Jeep in the school parking lot for a week?"

"Five days. No one'll bother it."

"What if I need a backup car?" The mask was dropping again. "You know, Matt, you may be a big cheese on the team, but you're still part of this family, living in my house, eating my food, driving a car leased to Rydek Catering. You're on my payroll."

Matt said nothing. He felt himself shrinking, hating the helpless feeling. For a moment, the only sounds in the kitchen were Romo's whimpers. Then Mom said, "We'll work it out."

"I'm sure you will." Dad marched out. Over his shoulder, he said, "A good camp is the foundation of a good season. Remember that."

Remember this, thought Matt, imagining raising a middle finger to Dad's back.

FIVE

"Your father really cares about you, Matt." Then Mom added, "He cares about both his boys."

It sounded tacked on to Matt. He checked Junie in the Jeep's rearview mirror. He was fussing with Romo's collar and didn't seem to have heard. But you can never be sure what he picks up on, Matt thought. Retarded doesn't mean dumb.

Mom was cranking up. "It's just the way your father communicates. He's very direct. Sometimes that can be off-putting to people who don't understand him. He can even sound angry."

"Not angry," said Junie. "Just trying to scare you. To get his way."

Mom whirled around. "Who told you that?"

"Is that wrong?" Junie's voice trembled.

"I told him," said Matt quickly. "At the game, when he was ragging on the ump."

"You were right, Junie honey," said Mom. She lowered her voice. "You have to be careful what you say, Matt." Then she patted his knee. "Give your father a chance. He only wants the best for you."

He had heard this so many times that tuning it out was as easy as tapping the mute. He was feeling too good to let it get at him now. In a couple of hours he would be far away. He felt relaxed in the heat of the afternoon. He had cleared his head with a long run in the cool, sweet foothills a few miles from the house and then a giggly hour on the living room rug with Junie and Romo, watching cartoons and wrestling. Junie needed more physical activity. Once school starts and Junie's back at his part-time cafeteria job, Matt thought, he can hang out at football practice, run a little, lift a few light weights. Coach Mac would be cool with that.

"Amanda?"

That brought him back in a hurry. "What?"

"When does she get back?"

"Why?"

"You sound so defensive. Everything all right between you two?"

"Why do you say that?"

"Mother's intuition."

"She's back tonight." He was glad to swing into the

Heinzes' big circular driveway.

Brody was out back, at the pool, helping his mother grill burgers. She was wearing a bikini, as usual at home in the summer. In the winter she usually wore a black spandex workout suit that was somehow even sexier though less flesh showed. She didn't mind being stared at, but Matt tried not to be too obvious about it around Brody.

"A week at camp, I could go for that," Mrs. Heinz said, handing Matt's mom a glass of white wine.

"I don't think so," said Brody. "The gassers, the sleds, the two-a-days."

"Two-a-days," said Mrs. Heinz. "Remember those, Jody?" She rolled her eyes and raised her glass. Matt's mom giggled. She acted like a kid around Mrs. Heinz. It was embarrassing, especially when they made sex jokes they thought nobody else got, thought Matt. Brody never seemed to notice how his mom shook her booty. All-Brody could see only Brody. Or maybe he knew how to shut it out.

"The last decent meal for a while," said Brody, shoveling burgers onto a plate. He left a big one on the grill for Junie, who liked his well done.

"Larry might do a barbecue," said Matt's mom.

"Awesome," said Brody. "Tell him to bring those amazing jumbo shrimps."

Romo ran past, chased by the Heinzes' Yorkie, who

was yapping at her hind legs. Just once, thought Matt, act like a dog, Romo. Turn around and face that fat rat, you only outweigh him by seventy pounds, you could eat him for lunch. He'd run if you just looked at him hard. Don't be a pussy all your life, Romo.

Junie puffed along after the dogs, his arms quivering. Brody's mom threw her arms around Junie and hugged him tight. Matt tried not to imagine what that felt like.

Matt and Brody ate quickly while their moms chattered. Brody went inside to get his duffel bag, and Matt said good-bye to Junie, who looked sad.

"You didn't give me the spare keys," said Mom.

"I'm leaving the keys under the front seat," said Matt.

She looked confused. "I thought you were going to leave me both sets."

"Couldn't find the spares." He avoided her eyes. The spare keys were deep inside his own duffel bag, along with the flask of Captain Morgan, the Vicodin, the pills from Monty, and the cell phone you weren't supposed to bring to camp. You never give up your last set of car keys. Certainly not to Dad.

"Have a great camp." She hugged him and Brody.

"What about me?" Brody's mom gave him a squeeze. Good thing it was quick. He was aroused.

And then they were free, spinning out of the driveway.

"You got lucky last night," said Brody.

"Can't remember her name."

"Sarah Ringe. Terri thinks she was stalking you, got a master plan."

"Since when you talking to Terri?"

"Since last night," said Brody. "She asks a lot of questions. But she doesn't talk when her mouth's full." He rubbed the football on his lap. "Now all we got to think about is ball."

SIX

Most of the team was already on the bus by the time Matt and Brody pulled into the parking lot. It was a big, comfortable commuter bus this year, a good sign. The company owner, a booster who had once played for the Raiders, donated a bus only in seasons he thought they would have a winning team. Otherwise, they'd be riding in a yellow school junker.

Ramp was standing at the bus door, checking off names on a clipboard. He got off on those bossy captain's jobs, thought Matt. Ramp was wearing his big tan work boots, what he called his "queer crushers." Two of his linemen buddies were handing out bags of chips and cold cans of soda, courtesy of a local 7-Eleven, as guys heaved their duffel bags into the open baggage compartment. The coaches were off in a corner of the lot with the student managers loading equipment into a pickup.

"Last time we do this," said Brody. He sounded sentimental.

"Next time we'll do it in the Big Ten."

They slapped high.

Matt slipped his car keys under the seat. He hadn't fooled Mom with his lie about the lost keys. But she must have understood or she wouldn't have been willing to run a number on Dad in the first place, letting Matt drive to the bus, then getting Mrs. Heinz to take her later to pick up the car. And then to have it waiting for him in the lot when he came home at the end of the week. He felt a twinge of guilt. Mom had her hands full with Junie, all her PTA stuff, working for Rydek Catering, and putting up with Dad. C'mon, Matt, she married him.

Matt and Brody pulled their Adidas duffels, gifts from the area rep, out of the car and hoisted them onto their shoulders. They sauntered toward the bus. They'd timed it to be the last ones aboard. The triple seat in the back would be empty for them.

They were almost at the bus when a black Lexus SUV screeched up. A huge kid jumped out and hauled his bag out of the back. He slammed the hatch shut and shouted good-bye to the woman at the wheel. She looked like a mom to Matt. Kid would learn.

Ramp said something to the linemen, Boda and Hagen. They laughed. Linemen always laughed at Ramp's lame cracks. They shut up as the kid tossed the big bag over a wide shoulder as if it were a sack of popcorn. It was such a smooth move, all graceful muscle, that Matt felt the same twinge of excitement he felt watching Tyrell. Kid was an athlete. He walked toward them with a cocky little spring in his Timberland sandals, the straps flapping.

Matt stood near the bus door. "Who's that?"

"Chris Marin," said Brody. "Sophomore transfer."

"How you know him?"

"Coach asked me to throw to him last spring. He could start."

"You didn't tell me."

"I forgot." Brody could be trusted to forget anything that wasn't about him.

"The tight end from Bergen Central?"

"How'd you know?" said Brody.

"Ramp said something about him last night. I think he's worried."

"Should be. Kid's real fast for his size, good hands."

They slowed down to reach the bus at the same time as the kid and check him out. He was as tall as Ramp, about six four, and almost as wide and thick. As they heaved their bags into the belly of the bus, Matt noticed that the kid's bag was an Army duffel with the name Andrew Marin stenciled on.

"Hey, Brody." Chris Marin held up his huge hands for the ball.

Brody cocked, but before he could throw, Ramp

growled. "Let's go, new meat. On the bus."

Chris glanced back and forth between Ramp and Brody. For all his size and cocky body language, Matt thought there was something hesitant in his face. Same soft eyes as Junie and Romo.

Hagen fired a soda can at Chris's groin. It hit home, but Chris caught it one-handed. Must have hurt. All he said was "Thanks." Sarcastically.

Ramp said, "Thank your mother for me."

Chris's chest started to swell and his neck got red. Ramp's potato face broke apart in an ugly grin. He loved it when he got to people. He'd deck the kid right here, say he was doing it for Raider discipline. Maybe that's not a good idea, Matt thought. We could use a good tight end, especially if he can catch the ball.

Matt stepped in between them and held up his hands to Brody, who flipped the ball. Matt could hear air rushing out, probably from Chris, maybe from himself. He turned his back on Ramp and pressed the ball into Chris's chest. "Take this on the bus for me, new meat."

Chris hesitated. Matt winked and pushed him toward the door. Chris shrugged and clambered noisily up the metal steps, throwing a hard look over his shoulder at Ramp.

"Your project?" said Ramp.

"Just helping you load the bus," said Matt. He took his can and chips from Hagen and climbed aboard.

Chris was already sitting near the front with the freshmen and sophomores. At least he had enough sense for that. Matt thought there was something like gratitude in his eyes as he handed over Brody's ball. Don't get attached, kid. I don't need a project.

Matt nodded at the freshmen and sophomores, said hello to those he knew. By the middle of the bus he was tapping fists with juniors he hadn't seen all summer. Part of the captain's job was making sure players knew they could come talk to you. At least part of my job. Ramp was more the enforcer. Matt traded bitch slaps with the seniors.

In the back of the bus, sitting with Pete, Tyrell was grinning and wagging his head. "Way cool, Cap'n Matt."

Matt shrugged. He didn't want to make a big deal out of it.

Brody said, "I wouldn't get between those two guys."

"Nooo," said Tyrell. "Brody would run out of bounds."

"You lucky if you touch the ball this season," said Brody, laughing. It was almost impossible to upset Brody. One of his strengths as a quarterback.

Matt pushed Brody into their backseat. Plenty of time for dumb chatter, don't need to start now.

Brody wedged himself into a corner and stretched out his long legs. Matt took the other side.

"You girls happy back here?" Ramp loomed up.

"Now we are," said Tyrell in a falsetto. "Captain Potatohead's here."

Ramp didn't like that, but he never tangled with Tyrell. He turned to Matt. "You and the kid got something going?"

"Give him a chance, let's see what he's got," said Matt.

"Count on that." Ramp pushed past Hagen and Boda and took his seat, a double.

Pete said, "Ramp's got a hard-on for the new kid already?"

"We'll work it out on the field," said Matt.

The driver revved the engine and the coaches climbed aboard.

They were out of Nearmont, on the highway, when Coach Mac stood up in the front of the bus. "Listen up, gentlemen." His voice was clear and loud. By the end of camp it would be softer, raspier. "You are heading into Raider country now, a band of brothers going to eat, sleep, breathe football for the next five days. Your coaches will be putting you through the meat grinder, and if you make it—not everybody does—you will be a Raider."

Brody and Pete listened and nodded. Tyrell rolled his eyes and slipped on his headphones. Coach Mac didn't bother changing his little speeches from year to year. Matt waited until he finished the part about measuring life in timeouts and yards before he put on his own Nike headphones. He liked that measuring image. Not thinking too hard about anything but football. He felt lighter. He cranked up the volume on his iPod just enough to drown out the coach and the chatter on the bus. He started drifting off, toward a dark, warm swimming pool with someone who could have been Mandy, Sarah Ringe, or Mrs. Heinz.

The last thing he saw before he reached the pool was Coach Mac raising two fists and mouthing what must have been "Raiders Rule!"

SEVEN

The kids up front cheered as the bus pulled into the old Army base and they stampeded off, yelling. The seniors waited until the aisle was clear before they even stood up. Matt looked out a window. Nothing had changed. Good. Dark, piney woods surrounded a large field with goalposts. There were two tan wooden barracks buildings, each with a latrine and shower room; a mess hall; a half dozen small cabins; and a small redbrick administration building. Supposedly, this had been a secret training camp for Special Forces reserve units back in the 1960s. It was miles from the nearest town.

"Welcome to Afghanistan," said Tyrell.

Pete and Brody groaned and cursed, but Matt knew they were happy, too. Just us and ball.

Outside, in the hot, airless twilight, he felt the sandy soil crunching under his flip-flops and working its way into the soft skin between his toes. It was a comforting discomfort, the start of good, familiar pain.

Ramp was standing importantly with his clipboard at the baggage compartments, giving out bunk assignments. Everyone except the seniors would be in double-deckers on the barracks floor. The managers were handing out bags of sandwiches, fruit, cookies, and bottles of water. No hot meal tonight. Early sack-out, up at six A.M.

"Captain Rydek. Single in Barracks Two." Ramp grinned. They'd made it. Ramp would have the single in Barracks One. The singles had once been platoon sergeants' quarters. The other seniors would share doubles, old corporals' quarters. Being captain means a lot more to Ramp than to me, Matt thought. Ramp loved the power. Even thought he deserved it. Probably couldn't wait to start running the nightly games, especially Raider Pride Night.

Chris Marin was waiting for his assignment, his duffel bag on his shoulder, tapping a sandal impatiently. He had a cocky expression on his face, but Matt noticed he looked lost. No friends here. He thought about saying something but decided not to. Can't baby a football player. Got to learn to suck it up. He remembered coming here for the first time freshman year, feeling lost, trapped, even though he had friends. By the end of that first camp, after getting through Raider Pride Night, he had felt at home.

Managers dragged out the seniors' duffel bags. Ramp snapped, "Marin, caddy for Rydek and Heinz."

Chris did a slow turn. "What?"

"You deaf as well as stupid? Freshmen carry seniors' bags first night."

"I'm not a freshman."

Hegan and Boda came over grinning, smelling trouble.

Matt hoisted his bag on his shoulder. "Nobody touches this baby but me." He shoved Brody. "Let's go." He waited until Brody picked up his bag, then headed toward the barracks. He didn't look back.

"Texas Hold 'Em tonight, my room," said Brody. He was bunking with Pete.

The inside of the barracks looked the same, a huge room with two rows of double-decker bunks on a splintery floor. The shower room smelled damp and moldy. There were still no partitions between the toilets. At his first camp, Matt couldn't sit on a toilet while other guys were around. He waited until the middle of the night to go. By the second summer he could take a dump and hold a conversation. He got to like it.

He was glad to have a single, an escape from the endless jabbing chatter. Might even skip the poker game tonight. Brody and Pete were into it—they'd been watching poker on TV all summer and playing online. Ramp and Hagen played, too.

Matt picked at the food, listened to some tunes, dozed

as the twilight darkened. He could hear the younger guys yelling and tumbling around in the big room. Let them get it out, the last night they'll have any extra energy. The coaches will come and shut them down soon enough. He stretched out on the bed. A little early for sleep, but he felt tired, from last night, the booze, the bus ride. Someone tapped on his door, jiggled the knob. Glad I remembered to bolt it. Probably Brody, but wouldn't he have banged on the door? He felt himself slipping away.

A moment later, someone was banging. "Drop your cock, pick up your socks, it's a Raider morning." Sounded like Coach Kornbauer, the one they called Corndog behind his back.

Outside on the sandy old parade grounds, Matt jogged in place as the team stumbled out for the morning run. At first he stayed in the middle of the pack with Pete, Tyrell, and Brody. Then he remembered that while there was more air at dawn than at twilight here, you still needed to run near the front of the pack to feel it on your face. He led them to the front, where Ramp and the linemen were setting a slow pace.

"Too slow." Chris moved alongside Matt with a nice, easy stride for a heavyweight. Matt wondered if he had tapped on his door last night.

"He . . . your . . . bitch?" gasped Ramp.

"What's your problem?" said Chris. "Besides breathing."

Matt swallowed his laugh. Ramp was a captain, after all. But the meatbag couldn't jog and talk. Ramp cursed and dropped back a few steps.

Matt yelled, "Raider kick," and picked up the pace, leading the Back Pack past the linemen. Chris stayed with them. Tyrell glided alongside Matt. "Fre-quent Fly-er, let's show these white boys how to do it."

Side by side, they pulled away from the rest of the team, bringing their knees high, stretching out their stride, feeling their muscles cooking. They didn't need to talk. They finished the laps around the field so far ahead of the team, they had the bathroom to themselves and were first on the chow line.

"We in a hurry for this?" asked Tyrell as the managers dumped dry balls of scrambled eggs, blackened bacon, and burned toast on their trays. There was water, juice, milk, peanut butter and jelly, yogurt, protein powders, and vitamins on the tables.

Brody plopped down beside them. "You run like that again, only the Mafia kid touches the ball this season."

"Mafia kid?" said Matt.

"Ramp says Chris's old man's in the slammer for a contract hit," said Brody.

"Tyrell likes that," said Tyrell. "A gangster blocking for you is double pro-tection."

Pete and Patel sat down at the table, then Heller and Conklin, the other senior wide receiver and running back.

They all complained about the pace he'd set. It was only the first day. Out of the corner of his eye, Matt spotted Chris with his tray in the middle of the mess hall, looking for an empty seat. Matt was relieved when he sat down with some freshmen.

Coach Mac came by and dropped a hand on Matt's shoulder. "Way to go, Matt. Don't let 'em cruise. Offense meets right after breakfast. Got some new plays you'll like."

"More quarterback keeps this year, Coach?" said Brody.

"Dream on, Heinzie," said Coach Mac.

The meeting was in a corner of the field. Matt noticed that Chris sat apart from the junior varsity freshmen and sophomores, closer to the varsity. Coach Kornbauer, the offensive coordinator, had set up a large white plastic board on an easel. Ramp and the center, Villanueva, were holding it steady against a hot wind while Corndog marked Xs and Os. He was some kind of technical guru. Nobody on the team had ever come close to beating him in Madden football.

"Stay in the now," said Coach Mac. "We're gonna walk through these plays today so we can run them in pads tomorrow. I want to emphasize that we're all on the same page here, winning games. As a team. Coach K?"

Corndog called the play the Triplex Option Series. He tried to make it sound complicated, but it seemed to come down to the receivers, the tight end, and the running backs all faking until the quarterback released the ball. The fullback would block. The only real difference, Matt thought, was using the tight end as a primary ball carrier. Ramp had usually been used as a blocker. He wanted to run with the ball and catch passes, but he had hard, stiff hands.

"Okay, let's try option one," said Corndog. "Heinz, Rydek, Williams, Torelli. Chris Marin at tight end, Rampolski at fullback."

There was a gasp at that. Brody widened his eyes at Matt. Putting the kid ahead of Ramp was pretty radical.

On the snap, Matt went deep, Tyrell clutched an invisible ball to his chest, and Marin ran up the middle with the ball.

"That's the idea," said Corndog. "It's all about forcing the defense to make some wrong choices."

"Decent linebacker's gonna read it, stuff the tight end easy," said Ramp.

"Not if we do it right," said Corndog.

"Not if I do it," said Chris.

There were some jeers and whistles at that. Ramp puckered his lips and made a sucking sound.

They walked through a dozen plays before Coach Mac nodded at Corndog and waved over some linemen.

"No hitting, half speed," said Corndog. "Ramp, go to middle linebacker."

Brody faked a handoff to Pete before firing a short pass to Chris. Nice soft hands. Ramp roared in. Chris feinted left, then spun away, leaving Ramp standing like a fool, hands out.

Chris kept running, picking up speed down the length of the field. He cut and juked around linemen pounding the sleds, then crossed the goal line with the ball in one hand over his head. He moonwalked a few steps.

Ramp watched him, frozen. The coaches were laughing, but Tyrell was shaking his head at Matt. You don't make Ramp look bad. Captain Potatohead never forgets. Be a long camp for the kid.

EIGHT

By the end of the first day, Chris was the buzz of camp. He outran everyone except the senior backs, and he lifted with the linemen. His agility through the strings was unusual for someone his size. He was good, Matt thought, but he flaunted it as if he weren't so sure. Never walked when he could strut, never talked when he could shout. He ran drills like they were conference games, which pissed off the veterans who weren't in shape yet.

"Better get mustard for that hot dog," said Brody.

Ramp laughed a little too loudly. "And some tea bags."

Only Boda and Hagen snickered.

"That's over," snapped Tyrell.

"Who elected you?" said Ramp.

"Got to hand it to him," said Pete. "Puts out a hundred and ten percent."

"Puts out for you?" said Ramp, making a kissing sound.

"Least he showed up in shape," said Tyrell, pointing to the roll of flesh overlapping Ramp's shorts.

"You want a piece, little bro?" Ramp grabbed his crotch. "Tea for two."

"Water break," said Matt, throwing an arm across Tyrell and steering him away.

"Someday Tyrell is gonna take a piece of that fat cracker," said Tyrell.

"C'mon, man, we're a team," said Brody, catching up. "Don't let's fight over some new kid."

"Not about him," said Tyrell.

At dinner that night, Chris was the only one who seemed to have any energy. Or was he faking it, making a show? Matt remembered Dad pointing out woozy boxers on TV grinning and dancing to pretend they were still dangerous. Never let them know you're hurting. Matt watched Chris, wondering why the kid fascinated him. He was a prospect, all right, but there was something about him that made Matt uneasy.

Everybody crashed that night. Brody didn't even mention poker. Matt didn't remember falling asleep, and then it was morning, and the coaches were banging cans and ringing cowbells.

The second day, in pads, Hagen managed to drop Chris with a knee-high tackle. The kid went down hard on his shoulder. But he bounced right back up. Shook it off. Grinned. Didn't rub.

On the next play, Brody hit him with a little button-hook. Chris juked Hagen and Boda out of their shoes, left them looking stupid, and almost made the goal line before Ramp ran him out of bounds. Chris spun away from Ramp's shove and danced on the sideline. Corndog screamed at Chris to cut it out, to show some Raider class, but the other coaches were smothering laughs.

Before lunch, Coach Mac pulled Matt aside. "Tone him down." Like there was only one him in camp. "I don't want to break his spirit, but he's trying too hard."

"I'll talk to him."

Coach Mac looked at Matt sharply, as if he'd heard the reluctance in his voice. "Captain's job. You got a problem?"

"No."

"I know you can see the big picture." He put a hand on Matt's shoulder. "This kid can help you put points on the scoreboard. Block for you. Make it hard for defenses to key in on you and Tyrell. He isn't going to take anything away from you."

Which is why he didn't ask Ramp to talk to him, thought Matt. Kid's going to take Ramp's job on offense.

"We're all on the same page here," said Matt. "Winning games."

"What I want to hear." The coach slapped his butt. Coaches never hear your sarcasm unless they want to.

At lunch, Brody wanted to brag about the buttonhook

54

but Tyrell interrupted to ask Matt what Coach said.

"Wants me to tell the kid to chill."

Tyrell moved his hands to a rap beat. "Better tell / the kid to chill / if you don't want / the Ramp to kill."

Good advice. Ramp shot glares at Chris through the afternoon, daring him to put a move on. Ramp looked like a dog waiting for a hamburger, salivating for the chance to bite. Going to be interesting once we get into one-on-one drills, Matt thought. Better talk to Chris before the Raider Games start.

It was too late. As they staggered into the mess hall for dinner, Ramp clambered up on a table and shook his helmet overhead. "Senior Service tonight. Senior picks a freshman's name, to carry his tray to the table and bus it when he's done." He dropped the helmet into Hagen's hands and the lineman lumbered over to the senior table.

"How come Ramp's in charge of this?" said Pete.

Matt shrugged. "Not my thing."

Brody plucked a scrap of torn paper and read "Lee." A skinny little ninth-grader ran over, grinning.

Matt remembered doing this his first year, scared but proud to be part of the team. Wasn't so bad. In fact, the senior whose tray he carried got him started working out at Monty's gym. By the time Matt was a sophomore, he was on the juice.

Matt picked Brett Rogers, the kid brother of a running back who had graduated. Nearmont always seemed to have terrific black running backs. Brett hustled up as if he had been waiting all his life for this moment. "Hey, Matt."

"How's DuShayne doing at Marshall?"

"Great. Might start. You want chicken or lasagna?"

"Marin," said Ramp, before Matt could answer. The second time he called the name, the mess hall quieted. "Let's go."

Chris threw a lazy look over his shoulder at Ramp but he didn't move. "You know I'm a sophomore."

"It's your first year at camp. Grab a tray."

Chris didn't move. Nobody moved. Matt thought, I'm the one who should be moving. I'm a captain. The coach told me to talk to the kid. Have to do something. Right now. What?

"Move your ass." Ramp's voice boomed when he let it loose.

Matt knew what to do. He was inside the zone, that calm, hushed place where time stood still, where everything was clear. It was the same feeling he sometimes had in a game when the vibes were coming off Brody and he sensed without looking that the ball was heading right into his hands. He saw everything in the mess hall sharply; the team frozen, the coaches watching warily from their corner table.

He strolled across the mess hall. "Take a walk with me, Marin."

He turned his back on Chris and continued his stroll out of the mess hall. He wasn't absolutely sure Chris would follow him out until he heard footsteps behind him crunching over the sandy soil.

It was still hot and bright. He walked to the edge of the field before he turned. Chris was right behind him, grinning. "Ramp owes you one. I woulda smeared the queer."

"Don't be so sure." Matt kept his voice flat, low. "Coach wanted me to talk to you."

"What about?" Chris's shoulders came up, tense.

"You expect to make this team?"

"You kidding, I—"

"You make your own teammates look bad, they'll make sure you don't."

"How they gonna stop me?"

"Figure it out. You need people to watch your back in this game, not step on your ankle in a pileup."

Chris blinked. After a while, he said, "I'm nobody's bitch."

Matt relaxed. Got him. "Listen to your captains and your coaches. Lose that show-off shit. Pay your dues like we all did." He waited until Chris nodded, then punched his arm. "You're a football player, Chris. Let 'em bring it. You can take it."

He turned sharply and headed back to the mess hall. After a moment, he heard Chris's crunching footsteps hurrying to catch up. They walked into the mess hall together. It looked like no one had moved. Ramp was waiting, smirking. Like I went out and fetched his bitch. Fuck that. I'm no bitch, either.

Brett Rogers was standing where Matt had left him, on the chow line with an empty tray.

"Brett," snapped Matt. "Serve Ramp. Marin. Grab a tray. You serve me."

Chris had no trouble with that. "Chicken or lasagna, Cap'n Matt?" With a cocky flourish he threw a paper towel over his arm like a fancy waiter and carried the tray on upraised fingertips to the table. Matt noticed that the coaches and most of the players were laughing, but Ramp was staring in silence. Finally Ramp shook his head and gave Brett his order.

"Way to go," said Tyrell when he came back to the table. Pete gave him a thumbs-up.

He knew he should be feeling good, but his head hurt. Not his thing. He ate quickly and went back to his room for a Vicodin before the video session. He dug out his cell. A dozen messages, all from Mandy. Shit. He was deciding whether or not to call back when the cell vibrated. Her ID came up on the screen. Might as well get it over with. "Eighty."

"What's going on?"

He was confused. Why would she care about Ramp and Chris, even know about them? "The usual, two-a-days—"

"Don't. How could you—" She sounded like she'd been crying.

"What?"

"—embarrass me like that—"

"Like what?" Somebody was rapping on his door.

"—with a cheap slut—"

"What are you talking—" In mid sentence, he got it.

"Movie night. C'mon." Brody had his head in the room.

"Gotta go."

"You asshole." She hardly ever used that kind of language. "Don't you dare—"

"Later." He snapped the cell shut and buried it in his duffel.

"Mandy?" said Brody.

"Found out about what's-her-face."

"Always a mistake," said Brody, "to answer the phone here. You lose your edge."

"Don't worry about it." Matt led the way out of the barracks to the brick administration building. Have to deal with her when we get back from camp, he thought, but I don't even have to think about her now.

For a half hour the team watched a cassette of last season's worst blunders: dropped balls, busted plays, missed assignments. The AV guy had mixed in a sitcom laugh track and some movie comedy music. Some of it was pretty funny, especially the dumb expression on Hagen's face after blowing a block, watching the play stampede past him.

Brody shouted out, "Wait for me, Mr. Frodo."

Nobody was spared—Brody's interceptions, Tyrell's fumbles, a missed tackle by Ramp, and Matt, at safety, being dragged five yards by a ball carrier. It was a third-night ritual. Let off some steam. As usual, though, most of the worst mistakes were made by guys who had graduated.

When the lights came on, Coach Mac had a fire burning in a metal wastebasket. The other coaches stood in a semicircle behind him. Coach Mac held the cassette over the flames.

"Gentlemen, this is the past. To get to the future, we need to get past the past. We learn from it and rise from its ashes." He dropped the cassette into the wastebasket and stepped back as flames whooshed up. Matt knew the cassette had been doused in lighter fluid. The freshmen gasped.

Ramp jumped up. "Raiders Rule!"

They all stood up chanting, "Raiders Rule, Raiders Rule," until the flames died down and Coach Mac dismissed them.

Matt slipped out of the building a few steps ahead of the rest of the team and hurried back to the barracks. Someone called out to him, maybe Chris, but he needed to get away from them all, stretch out, take another Vic, maybe a pull on the flask. Too much was going on in his head. He was here for football, not jerk-off games. He just wanted to catch the ball and then let it carry him out of town. Why did he have to get involved with complications? Couldn't people leave him alone?

It's not always about you, Matt.

The sports psychologist had said that. The start of his junior year, when he dropped a few passes, Dad took him into the city to see a shrink who worked with the Giants. Dad had read about a visualization technique where you could raise the percentage of successful catches by imagining them. But Dad never got a chance to tell the shrink what he wanted. He had to sit outside in the waiting room, steaming, while Matt had his session. Matt had sort of liked the guy. He had a soft voice and wore glasses, but from the size of his neck you could see he had lifted, been a jock. He understood.

He had patients, the shrink said, no names but you would recognize them, who suddenly couldn't execute. They missed blocks they always made, dropped passes they always caught. Usually it was a signal from deep inside, something's wrong, get me out of here. You need to find out what's going on.

Matt listened to him, but what could he say? There was so much he didn't want to talk about all jumbled in his head. Hating Dad for being on his back to give up baseball and concentrate on football and feeling guilty because

61

he knew Dad loved him in his own way, especially because of Junie. Remembering how he used to wish Junie would die so he would get some attention and then feeling guilty for that and trying to make it up to Junie. Pushing himself harder in the gym helped blot out those thoughts, and then when that wasn't enough, the booze and the Vics helped. He certainly didn't want to talk about the steroids. Monty was still tinkering with the dosage, and there were days when Matt went from sad to mad in ten seconds. Monty had warned him about 'roid rage, and he'd managed to keep it under control, especially when driving. Came close to decking a coach once, and very close to slapping Terri. He and Terri were the class couple then. She was always trying to get into his head, talk about feelings, about their relationship. It felt like she was trying to strip off his skin. He even lost interest in fooling around with her. Never any problems with Mandy. No touchy-feely questions. Either she understood, or she didn't care. Either way was fine. They were sex machines.

But he couldn't get any of it out, shifted in his chair, mumbled about losing concentration in games. After a while, the psychologist had sighed and said that they could do this slowly. Meanwhile, think about this: You get so much attention, you're under so much pressure from your family, coaches, teammates, people in the community, college recruiters, you start to think you are responsible for everything. The sun's up, you're welcome, folks.

It's raining, sorry about that. Give yourself a break, Matt. It's not always about you. Especially the bad stuff. You need to take some real deep breaths when you feel the world closing in on you. Matt wanted to ask him how he knew about that, but the shrink said, "That's all we have time for today."

The shrink called Dad in and talked to both of them. Said he thought it would be a good idea if Matt came in once a week for a while, and talked on the phone at least once a week, too. Dad said he would think about it, but on the drive home he exploded, called the guy a quack. Dad said the shrink knew Matt was a winner and he wanted to get on the gravy train early, screw with his head, get control. This is a quick-fix situation and this hustler's looking for a long-term payoff.

Never saw the shrink again. Monty found the steroid combo that worked and Matt broke up with Terri. Never dropped another pass.

Wonder how the shrink would deal with Chris and Ramp.

NINE

The third and fourth days at camp went quickly, as they always did. They were the busiest, the hardest, and in some ways the most fun. The players were starting to understand the new plays even if they couldn't always execute. The pains of the first two days had settled into the dull aches that would remind them all season they were football players. And they were hitting now, which was what the game was all about.

On the fourth day, Chris went up against Ramp one-on-one for the first time. No contest. Ramp hit low and hard and came up with Chris on one shoulder like a matador speared on a bull's horn. Everybody winced when Chris hit the ground. He didn't bounce up, but he didn't rub. He said something to Ramp they couldn't hear, but it wiped the smirk off Ramp's face.

The second time they collided, Ramp was too eager.

He drove Chris backward, but he couldn't knock him down. Ramp glowered as Chris walked away, smiling. Chris had toned down the hotdogging, but he could get Ramp steamed just by making a good move.

Matt avoided them both. There was plenty to do. He worked hard, running, lifting, paying attention at meetings. A captain is a role model. You don't always have to be on people's backs. You can just be. Show them. The younger players would come hunching up, shyly or with bravado, to ask questions—Did he use stickum? Did the new face masks obscure his vision? What about bump and run?—but it was really to see if he would blow them off. They wanted to be sure he'd be there for them if they ever had a real problem. He listened carefully and tried to answer their questions. If they asked for advice, he would tell them to concentrate, not to let anything distract them, to keep their eyes on the ball. They nodded seriously at that, made him feel like Obi-Wan Kenobi.

He could always concentrate, could shut out the distractions, the noise from the sidelines, the waving banners, the stray thoughts that could snag like plucking fingers. Dad, Ramp, Mandy, Chris: bury them all deep in the duffel bag. Think ball. Learn the new plays, make the new routes automatic, home in on the vibes off Brody, the ball a heat-seeking missile locked on his hands. Brody was complaining that the new plays gave him too much to think about, three primary targets instead of two, but

Matt figured he really wanted more chances to run with the ball. Corndog didn't like Brody scrambling. He said that's when bad things happened, injuries, lost yardage, turnovers.

The defensive backfield coach, Dorman, a young guy, had come up with some new pass coverage ideas. More to learn. That was good. Keep the mind as tired as the body. Matt liked playing safety on defense because it reminded him of centerfield, the last chance to stop a score.

Casually, during a water break, Dorman asked Matt if he had ever thought about moving to cornerback.

"I think you'd have a better shot at the NFL as a corner than a receiver," said Dorman. "Try it out here—you might think about making the switch in college. Your grades and all, you could get a Big Ten ride as a corner like that." He snapped his fingers.

He liked wide receiver, liked catching the ball. What would Dad think about that? If he was against the idea, he'd be on Dorman like a dog on a bone. Coach Mac was probably behind the idea but was letting Dorman take the heat. Would Coach Mac have Dorman mention it to Dad when he came out for the barbecue? Was the barbecue even going to happen? No word yet. Put it out of your mind, Matt. Too much stuff going on, all those plucking fingers. Concentrate.

He spent a lot of time with Coach Sims, who was working with quarterbacks and wide receivers. He'd been an all-conference wide receiver at Wisconsin and lasted two years in the NFL on special teams before he got hurt and cut. He worked on Matt's mechanics, his start and the position of his hands while running. He made Matt run the same receiving route a dozen times before he was satisfied.

"Muscle memory," he said. "You can't be thinking about it. Mind got to be clear for the unexpected."

When Coach Dorman whistled Matt over for defensive drills, Coach Sims held up five fingers for a few more minutes. Dorman looked annoyed but Sims had more clout with Coach Mac. Two years in the League was a heavy résumé.

"Coach Dorman talk to you about switching to corner for college?" When Matt nodded, Sims said, "You got to do what feels right. You're a real good receiver, good instincts, good hands."

"You switched."

"Got switched. So hungry to play pro, I let it happen." Sims shook his head. He was the only black coach among the five in camp. "A little more confidence, a better agent, I might still be in the League, catching the rock. You could use another twenty pounds. Receivers are getting bigger."

"Twenty pounds'd slow me down."

"Not if you put 'em on right." Coach Sims didn't look at him. Coaches never looked at you when they were pretending they weren't talking about steroids. How else you going to pack on twenty pounds of muscle quickly? Don't ask, don't tell.

Something else he didn't want to think about right now. He wouldn't be playing both ways in college. Most of the recruiters were promising a slot at wide receiver, not starting as a freshman but high on the depth chart. But you can't ever be sure what happens once they get you there.

Another twenty pounds? Would have to up the dosage. Ask Monty about that. Monty would talk to Dad. His money. Matt had never talked to Dad directly about steroids, but he knew Dad and Monty sometimes hung out and he figured they talked about it. Two years on steroids and he liked the way he felt now. Strong, big, up. Sure, there were a few pimples on his shoulders. Now and then a sudden flush of anger. But that usually happened when Dad pissed him off. Could happen if he was shooting Gatorade.

By the afternoon of the fourth day, it was clear that Dad wasn't showing up with a Rydek barbecue. Matt was relieved and disappointed. He hated the way Dad grab-assed with the coaches like he was one of them. But the barbecue also seemed like just another half promise that wasn't kept. Had he dangled the possibility of it to tease him?

Nobody mentioned it. Wasn't missed. Even Brody

had forgotten about the jumbo shrimp. Dinner was just a fuel stop, the end of the physical part of the day, stuff down enough food to fill the holes and try to stay awake through the after-dinner meetings. Close your eyes only during the videos. Everybody was whipped and sore. Head crammed with information.

The air never seemed to cool off here, the sandy soil holding the heat of the day into the night, a dry wind moving it around like a kitchen fan.

The coaches disappeared into their cabins after the team meetings. They had their own meetings. Or maybe they were drinking and watching pornos. A couple of them would reappear at lights-out to take a head count.

There were always stories of guys on past teams who had girls waiting in cars on the other side of the woods, but they were probably just stories. Too tired. The Back Pack had trouble concentrating on its poker games in the double Brody and Pete shared. The games broke up early.

Pete had followed Matt out of the room on the third night. "Maybe you should call Mandy."

"Why?"

"Lisa says she's really hurt. You should reach out."

"What am I gonna say? I'm sorry? Never happen again?"

"Make her feel better," said Pete. "Even if it's not true."

"Don't do it," said Brody. He had followed them out.

"Lose concentration. When Terri starts that stuff, I hang up."

"I thought you weren't answering your phone," said Matt.

"Could be my brother," said Brody.

"Caller ID?"

Brody changed the subject. "You know Rydek Catering lost the quarter final?"

So that was why no barbecue. The old man wasn't coming out to camp a loser.

Ramp wanted the Back Pack to attend his Raider Games, but they weren't in the mood. Matt checked in briefly because it seemed like something a captain should do. They were silly and harmless, the usual, making the freshmen sing, stagger blindfolded through obstacle courses of garbage, find the statue of a snarling catamount, the Eastern Valley High mascot, that had been hidden in the woods. The freshmen stumbled through the woods in the dark, wearing only helmets, jockstraps, and shoes, while sophomores and juniors hid behind trees and made animal noises.

Matt remembered he'd liked the camaraderie of the Raider Games his freshman and sophomore years, but by junior year he was bored.

Chris showed up for the games, did what he was supposed to do, and Ramp left him alone, practically ignored him. Matt wondered if he was really cutting the kid slack or setting him up. Ramp was tricky. Matt sensed that Chris wasn't sure what was happening either. Matt caught Chris looking at him a few times like he wanted to talk but was waiting for Matt to make the first move again. Let him wait. Or ask. I'm Captain Matt, not Dr. Phil.

But at practice, the kid was still pushing hard. Coaches' pet. He volunteered to hold for Patel's kicks, and he even tried his leg at field goals. Not bad. He was mowing down the sophomore and junior linemen on one-on-ones. The coaches didn't match him with Ramp again, but they put him in with Hagen. Chris ran over him and Ramp gave him a thumbs-up. That wasn't Ramp's style, Matt thought. Chris better watch out. But the kid just grinned.

Everybody went all out the fifth day. Final chance to make an impression. The season opened in a week, and the starting lineup was taking shape in the coaches' minds. Last day was always as dangerous as the first. Hamstrings pull, shoulders pop. Villanueva went down with a possible broken wrist. A trainer drove him back to Nearmont for X-rays.

At dinner, Coach Mac congratulated them on a good camp.

"Last time we hear this speech," said Brody sadly.

"I have high hopes for this team." Coach Mac's voice was low and raspy after five days of shouting. "I found out this week that you gentlemen have the *skill* to be football players. This season we'll find out if you have the *will* to be Raiders. To get back up when you've been knocked down. To put out when you're hurting. To suck it up and soldier on when everybody else thinks you're beaten."

Coach Mac took a deep breath, and Tyrell whispered, "If you can be a football player and a Raider, you know you're going to be one helluva man."

Brody glared at Tyrell.

"If you can be a football player and a Raider," said Coach Mac, "you know you're going to be one helluva man. No meetings tonight. On Raider Pride Night, your captains are in charge."

The assistant coaches followed him out. Ramp swaggered to the center of the mess hall. He grinned at Chris and then at Matt. The food in Matt's stomach suddenly felt like a hard, cold lump.

TEN

Trailed by the linemen, Ramp stomped around the mess hall, rapping a little white plastic bat on the tables and chairs he wanted them to clear away to the corners of the big room. Sheets were hung over the windows, the lights dimmed. Waving the bat, Ramp ordered the freshmen to the center of the mess hall and told them to strip to their underpants. The rest of the team crowded in a semicircle around them.

The freshmen stood shoulder to shoulder in a line, grinning and jiggling nervously as linemen tied their hands behind their backs with cord. Ramp was following the script. When he asked Matt to read "A Letter from No. 75," Matt relaxed. The little white bat had him worried for nothing. It was the same old same old.

"Dear Mom, Dad, Grandma, Sis, and Buddy," Matt read. He almost knew the letter by heart. He avoided looking at Tyrell, who would be mouthing the words and trying to make him laugh. The letter was supposedly from a soldier writing home from somewhere in Europe during World War II. His platoon was resting after a firefight, and the reason they came through it was because of the discipline and unit solidarity No. 75 had learned playing Raider football. Tyrell claimed that a cousin of his in South Carolina had heard the same letter.

> *I've got to stop now, folks—we're saddling up. Sarge won't tell us where we're going. But I know that when we get there, we'll be all right. We're a band of brothers and we watch each other's backs. I learned about that from my coaches at Nearmont High. I'll be back to thank them after we win.*
> *Love, Mike.*

When Matt finished reading, Ramp took the paper back and read, "That letter Captain Matt just read to you is more than sixty years old. But it could have been written by a Raider fighting for his country in Korea, Vietnam, Kuwait, Somalia, Iraq, anywhere a warrior depends on his teammates when the going gets tough." He lowered the paper and searched the semicircle around him until he found Chris. "Anyone else here who has never been initiated into the Raider brotherhood?"

In the dim light, Matt sensed more than saw the confusion on Chris's face. What does he do now? Still say he's not a freshman, or step forward? The kid was afraid to put himself in Ramp's hands, but he wanted to be part of the team.

Ramp said, "Is there anyone else here who wants to show his brothers he's man enough to be a Raider?"

Chris looked around until he found Matt. Chris's eyes were wide. He's waiting for a signal from me.

Matt nodded. Let 'em bring it. You can take it.

Ramp saw it all. He gave Matt a thumbs-up and nodded at Chris.

Chris stood up and stepped forward. He stripped down to his shorts and held his hands behind his back as Boda tied them. He was grinning as he took his place with the freshmen.

Ramp said, "All sophs and juniors out of here."

"They didn't send anyone out last year," said Pete.

Ramp locked the door after the sophs and juniors left. "Blindfolds for the rookie Raiders. It's tea bag time."

"Thought no more of that shit," said Tyrell.

"Least it's not swirlies," said Brody.

"What you gonna do, Cap'n Matt?" said Tyrell.

"Be okay," said Matt. But he wasn't sure. "We're here."

Should I do something now?

But what?

He felt suddenly small, the way Dad could make him feel small. Powerless.

Just before the rags were tied around the rookies' eyes, Ramp, Boda, and Hagen dropped their pants and underwear and cupped their genitals in their hands.

"On your backs." Ramp rapped the bat against his bare leg. "Open your mouths for the dipping of the tea bags."

Still nothing new here. Matt remembered his own fear and disgust freshman year when he was tea bagged, the relief and laughter afterward when he'd realized that he'd been slapped in the face with a boiled hotdog and a leather sack of little rubber balls. He, Brody, and Pete had become even closer after going through that together.

But there was something in Ramp's voice. . . .

The linemen moved among the bodies, dangling the little bags and the hotdogs into the upturned faces. Some of the kids gagged, tried to turn their heads; one began to whimper.

Ramp, Hagen, and Boda chanted, "Tea bag, tea bag, tea bag."

The other seniors pushed forward to watch. Some were laughing.

"Ready to kiss the tea bag, hotshot?" Ramp stood over Chris. He was naked from the waist down. He whacked the bat against his leg.

Abruptly, he squatted and dropped his groin into

Chris's face. Urine squirted out, into Chris's mouth and nose.

There was a choking sound, then Chris kicked up at Ramp, catching him on the thigh.

"You cunt," roared Ramp, jumping back. He kicked Chris in the ribs, then dropped down on him, knees first into his chest, driving the air out of him.

Chris fought to get up. He heaved Ramp off, then rolled over on his knees, still blindfolded, his hands tied behind him.

"I'm gonna get my gun and blow your fucking head off," Chris yelled.

Ramp leaped on Chris's back, drove him flat into the floor. "You're shit on a stick, wiseguy, shit on a stick."

Ramp pulled down Chris's underpants. Roaring, his muscles bulging, Ramp plunged the white bat deep into him.

Chris screamed.

Matt tried to move, felt paralyzed.

Tyrell said, "Motherfucker," and hurled himself through the linemen surrounding Chris and Ramp. Matt and Pete followed him, pushing through the freshmen, still blindfolded, tied, looking scared.

Vomit rose into Matt's throat.

Chris was on his knees again, shaking, his tied hands trying to reach down to the bat sticking out of him. Blood trickled down one leg.

Tyrell pulled out the bat and threw it away. In the sudden silence, he looked over his shoulder at Ramp. "You crazy?"

"It's Pride Night," said Ramp.

"You crossed the line." Tyrell lunged at Ramp, but Matt got between them.

"He needed it," said Ramp. "Asked for it."

"We don't do this shit," said Tyrell.

"Like you people know."

Tyrell went straight for Ramp's throat, screaming, "You cracker," but hands pulled him back. Matt put his palms on Ramp's chest, expecting resistance, but the big lineman just grinned at him.

"What's the big deal? You gave the okay, Cap'n Matt."

Matt felt frozen, tongue-tied. What's he talking about?

Pete helped Chris to his feet and gently steered him through the silent semicircle toward the mess hall door.

"Figures," said Ramp.

"What?" Matt's tongue was unstuck, but dry and thick.

"Missy Chrissie and Tweety Petey, two of a kind." Ramp snapped his fingers at Boda and Hagen. "Turn the rookies loose. Have 'em clean up. Show's over."

"Just starting, shithead," said Tyrell. "You're gonna get fried for this."

"Shut the fuck up," said Ramp. "Everybody better shut the fuck up."

78

"Let's go," said Brody. He grabbed Tyrell and Matt and pulled them toward the door. Matt let himself be pulled, and he saw Tyrell did, too.

What do we do now? he thought.

Pete was waiting for them outside the mess hall. It was dark, but still airless and hot.

"He took off after I untied him," said Pete. "Said he wanted to be by himself."

"Better find him," said Tyrell.

"Then what?" said Brody.

"Be sure he's not hurt bad," said Tyrell.

"Or hurt himself more," said Pete.

"You think?" said Matt.

"He was fucked up," said Pete. "Cursing and crying. What should we do?"

They were all looking at Matt. "Which way'd he go?" Matt said.

"Toward the woods," said Pete.

"Never find him," said Brody.

"Gotta try," said Matt.

They searched for hours, rarely speaking except to shout, "Chris, Chris," the sound muffled by the low branches that whipped their heads and shoulders. It seemed like a waste of time to Matt, yet they had to do it. Gotta try, pushing on, numb and tired and feverishly hot. He could tell they all felt the same way. Should we have stopped it, he thought, could we have? We? Me.

They didn't actually quit searching. Around midnight, they just followed a trail out of the woods and stumbled back into the clearing. The barracks lights were out.

"His bunk's in Ramp's barracks," said Pete. In the silence, he said, "I'll look."

They waited outside while Pete went inside.

"What'd Ramp mean by Tweety Petey?" said Brody.

"He's trying to split us up," said Tyrell.

"Gotcha," said Brody, but Matt wondered if he did understand. Wonder if I do, he thought.

Pete came out shaking his head. "Never showed up."

"He could have got to the highway and hitched a ride," said Tyrell. "Now what?"

They were looking at Matt again. He said, "If he doesn't show by morning when we leave, we'll have to tell a coach."

"Tell 'em what?" said Brody.

"In the morning," said Matt. "Let's get some sleep."

"Yeah, right," said Pete.

ELEVEN

He didn't expect to fall asleep, even with an Ambien. He couldn't delete the image of Chris on his knees, shaking, his tied hands trying to reach down to the bat sticking out of him as blood trickled down his leg.

Okay, he thought, you can't change it, get past it.

You going to get all twisted up because you gave him the okay to go ahead? Who knew it would get out of hand, that Ramp really was going to tea bag him, then go nuts?

Should have known. Ramp's been an asshole and a bully since PeeWee, and if you hadn't stood up to him, then he'd be pushing you around now. For ten years, mostly playing on the same teams, you've stayed out of each other's faces. One more season and you'll never have to deal with him again.

But what about this season, what about what he did to Chris? In front of you? A captain.

C'mon, worse things happen in a game.

Like what?

Chris was waiting by the bus with his duffel bag when the team assembled for the ride home. He was pale, hunched over. He didn't talk to anybody or make eye contact. Matt thought about saying something to him, slapping his shoulder, but decided not to. He seemed to want to be left alone. He sat up front near the coaches, who avoided looking at him. What did they know?

The ride home was quiet. It was usually rowdy, guys ranking on each other, new friends after five days. This time, they all seemed lost in their music. The seniors and freshmen were particularly quiet, but even the sophomores and juniors knew something had happened. The coaches made more noise than the players, as if they were trying to make up for the silence. They must suspect something, thought Matt. But they didn't really want to know. Like steroids—don't ask, don't tell. There could be trouble over this. Hurt the team.

A few miles out of town, Pete climbed over Tyrell, who looked like he was pretending to sleep, and leaned over Brody, who was asleep. "What are we going to do?" said Pete.

Matt thought, We're going to shut the fuck up, but he said, "We'll see."

Pete nodded. It seemed to satisfy him, and he climbed back over Tyrell, who opened one eye, stared at Matt, and closed it slowly.

The head manager stood up to remind them to wear clean Raider T-shirts to the Welcome Home pep rally tonight. He didn't get the usual hoots, just low muttering. Nobody was in the mood to be welcomed home.

Car horns honked as the bus pulled into the school parking lot. Friends, brothers, girlfriends, a few moms and sisters of the freshmen and sophs were waiting. The black Lexus SUV was there, and Chris was in it before the Back Pack climbed down from the bus. Matt's Jeep was there, too. Good old Mom. He bumped fists with Pete and Tyrell, nodded as the coaches said, "Good camp, rally tonight, practice tomorrow morning," and grabbed his bag. Brody caught up with him at the Jeep, but he didn't say anything until they were rolling.

"So whatcha gonna do?" said Brody.

"I don't know."

"You better have a plan."

"Why does it have to be me?" It came out angry.

"You leave it to them, Matt, they'll team up and barbecue your balls."

"What are you talking about?"

"Mandy and Sarah, man. You on another planet?"

Sometimes you'd think Brody was on another planet, Matt thought. "We got other problems."

"Like?" Brody made a comic face.

Matt laughed. Brody was laughing, too. Maybe he

wasn't on another planet. Maybe there was nothing else to do right now.

Brody said, "Wanna come in, catch the Yankee game?" They were pulling into his big circular driveway.

"I'm whipped. Gonna rack. Need a ride to the rally?"

"Nah. See you there." He dropped out of the Jeep.

Matt glimpsed Mrs. Brody coming out of the house in her bikini, and he pulled out fast. Didn't want to deal with anybody.

He was glad to find his own house empty. Mom had left a note on the refrigerator.

> *Welcome back, Matt! The chicken is*
> *for dinner, hands off! Shakes on the top*
> *shelf. Went to pick up Junie. See you at*
> *the rally. Love, Mom.*

He chugged a protein shake while he whizzed in the downstairs bathroom, then wandered the house, enjoying the air-conditioning, the comfort of the rooms. The desk in Dad's den was stacked with college brochures, videos, CDs, letters, and e-mails from coaches and varsity alumni explaining why Matt and their school were a perfect fit. The shelves on the walls were filled with softball trophies. *Rydek Catering isn't getting one this year,* Matt thought. *That's okay with me.*

He went upstairs, dumped his bag on the bed, and

glanced at Jerry Rice. Wonder what he would have done on Pride Night.

He put on running shoes, shorts, and a singlet, grabbed his iPod and car keys, and went out again. He could taste the end of summer in the afternoon air. The fading sweet smell of flowers and vines mixed with the distant silvery edge of fall. He'd always loved this time of year, just before the football season. All the good times lay ahead, excitement right around the corner, a fresh start, the possibility that this year would be different, better. He'd felt some of that expectation hooking up with new girls, even once or twice with new classes. But nothing like the thrilling expectation of a new season. Something in the pit of his stomach made him wonder about this new season.

He was driving before he realized he had left his cell phone home. On purpose? No one he wanted to talk to. He drove out of town and parked the Jeep in the public lot at the foot of the trail. Few other cars. He slipped on the headphones and found a pounding beat he thought would drive out everything else. He stretched before starting up the narrow dirt path.

He concentrated on the twists of the trail, the music, and his breathing, but the fingers kept plucking at the corners of his mind. Chris, Dad, Ramp, Mandy, Sarah, Junie. He couldn't quite run them off.

The house was still empty when he got back. Pete and

Brody had left messages on his cell phone. Just checking in. Four messages from Dad. He erased them without listening to them. A girl left her number. She said it was a new one. Could have been Sarah Ringe. He tried to remember what she looked like. There were three click offs from private numbers. He didn't want to think who that could be.

TWELVE

The Welcome Home rally seemed quieter than in past seasons, Matt thought, but maybe that was just in his mind. He stood with the Back Pack in the middle of the seniors on the platform in front of the grandstand. The rest of team was on the grass around them. Chris wasn't there. Be surprised if he was, Matt thought. Mandy was up front with the cheerleaders. She made a show of turning her back on Matt.

Brody caught the move. He elbowed Matt. "Jewelry. Worked for Kobe."

"They were married."

"You want to keep tapping that ass, right?"

There were at least two hundred people in the stands. He spotted Dad, Mom, and Junie in the front row. A Rydek Catering van was parked nearby. They'd be handing out lemonade and cookies afterward. Good for business, Dad always said.

Coach Mac welcomed the crowd, then turned the cordless mike over to Pastor Jim, the team chaplain. He was the youth minister at the Rydeks' church. Matt had never liked him, another adult with all the answers. His lips brushing the mike, Pastor Jim asked God to give the Raiders the strength to get back up when they were knocked down, to forgive cheap shots, and to win clean. He closed his eyes and asked the crowd to beam special energy to the young warriors representing them.

When Pastor Jim opened his eyes, he turned to the seniors. "Your last season here, be proud of your team, make your team proud of you. Be bigger than the game. Brody, next time you pass that pigskin, put a little extra spiral on it for the kids who look up to you." Brody waved to the crowd. "And Matt, you and Pete and Tyrell run just a little faster for them. You know, if Jesus came back, he'd be a Raider, hitting hard and hitting clean, linebackers like Ramp and Curt and Donny and José. He'd be kicking the money changers the way Jay kicks the ball. All of us, and that certainly means you, Ted and Kevin and Troy and Reggie and Tariz and Marquis and Michael, we have to turn it up a notch in our daily lives, crank the amps for ourselves and for those who need us." He signaled someone to hand up his guitar. "I'm going to ask some members of the Nearmont High School Select Chorus to join me now in the song 'Climb With Me.'"

Five kids came up on the platform behind Pastor Jim. Matt spotted Sarah Ringe immediately, as good-looking as he remembered. *So I wasn't that wasted,* he thought. Pastor Jim strummed a few bars and they began to sing, voices strong and clear even up against the noise of cars moving in and out of the lot. A tall, fat boy he had seen in the football marching band sang the first solo; then Sarah's high voice sent a shiver down his spine.

> *Take my hand and we will lead*
> *Each other up the highest hill*
> *Trust the Lord and teach it*
> *Together we can reach it*
> *If you take my hand and climb with me.*

He sneaked a glance at the cheerleaders. Mandy was glaring at Sarah. *Better do something before they team up. Barbecue my balls.*

Coach Mac took back the mike and introduced all the seniors again. Matt could hear Junie shouting when his name was called. The mayor came up and said something, and a few other town big shots, but their voices faded. Matt thought he saw Chris standing alone behind the wire fence in a far corner. He blinked sweat out of his eyes and Chris was gone. Had he ever been there?

Pastor Jim ended the rally with a prayer for a successful, injury-free season. Matt felt numb. When it was over, he followed Pete off the platform, staying in the middle of the Back Pack until they passed the cheerleaders.

"Matt?" It was the *Nearmont Eye* reporter he had blown off at the softball game, still hopping up and down like a frog. "What do you think?"

"About what?" What did the frog know? Had he talked to Chris?

"What Pastor Jim said about Jesus. You think he'd be a Raider?"

"That's Pastor Jim. We just play our game." It sounded dumb. What was this kid after?

He was glad when Junie yelled and waved him over to the Rydek van. Mom and Junie were handing out cookies and drinks. Romo was asleep under the truck, and Dad was working the crowd. It took Matt ten minutes to walk off the field. People kept stopping him. People always liked to tell him stuff so they could be seen talking to him, mostly compliments, good wishes for the season, sometimes jokes and gossip. He usually liked it, but tonight he felt tense, ready to break and run. Was he nervous that someone would ask about Chris? Ask what?

Someone asked him if he'd heard that the cops had found a marijuana stash in a gym locker and burned it. Rumor was the pot belonged to a football player. Matt shrugged and moved on.

Dad grabbed his arm. "Called you this afternoon, Matt."

He shook free. "Long run."

"Football season, not track." He looked angry.

He felt like walking away. Dad wouldn't make a fuss here. Pay for it later, but that's later. Always got to pay the price, hoss. He was making his decision when Junie handed him a bottle of water. "Gotta stay hylated, right, Mattie?"

"Hydrated," snapped Dad. "Long runs stretch the wrong muscles."

"Coach says we need to build stamina for the fourth quarter." It sounded like something Coach Mac would say.

"Pull a hammie and then what?" Dad raised his voice. "Scout from Penn State is coming to see you play."

"Nittany Lions," said Junie.

"Mr. Rydek? I'm Sarah Ringe." Matt didn't see her until she was shaking Dad's hand and he was trying to look down her white chorus blouse. "You catered my father's fiftieth birthday party. It was fabulous."

"Lovely affair." Matt could tell Dad was trying to remember. "Do you know my son Matt?"

"We've met." So cool the way she turned and smiled at him. "And I certainly know Junie." She squeezed Junie's arm. "My parents thought you were the best server at the party."

Junie beamed and hugged her hard.

"Easy there," snapped Dad.

"We're friends," said Junie, hugging harder. Matt

could see Sarah was trying to keep smiling as Junie squeezed the air out of her.

"You hear me?" shouted Dad.

"How about a group hug?" said Matt. He circled them both with his arms and pried Junie's arms loose. Junie grinned, and Sarah took a quick breath and gave him a grateful look.

Mom came over, checking Sarah out with narrowed eyes. "You have a lovely voice."

Romo woke up and slouched over to press against Sarah's leg.

Brody marched up and slapped the ball into Matt's gut. "Let's roll. Monty's waiting."

Dad said, "Tell him to call me."

On the ride to the gym, Brody said, "Those chicks gonna fight it out for you."

"Right."

"Terri says Sarah's locking in on you."

"How come you're suddenly talking to Terri so much?"

"You know, she's an interesting—"

"Talk about something else or just shut the fuck up."

"Somebody sucked a sour dick. Okay, how about the big pot bust?"

"I thought they just found some in a locker."

"A football player's locker," said Brody. "You think it's Tyrell?"

"Why should I think that?"

"He goes back and forth to the city, he's a head, and he doesn't juice with us."

"That's the same crap Ramp tried to lay on him last year, and we didn't buy it."

"Whatever."

At the gym, Ramp and the linemen were already at the racks by the time the Back Pack was dressed and out on the floor. They were barking and yelping, humping major weight in the last push before the season began. It would be harder to keep lifting heavy while trying to heal from the pounding of games.

"Yo, bro," yelled Ramp at Tyrell. "Hope you got paid for that weed."

"Burn, baby, burn," yelled Hagen. "Cops said it was primo."

"You start that again, better be ready to finish it," said Tyrell, making fists.

Matt put a hand on Tyrell's shoulder. "Gotta work now."

Matt kept the Back Pack on the machines until the linemen finished with the freeweights. He held them at the racks until Ramp and his elephants clumped out of Monty's office with their little postshot smirks. Nothing like feeling you were getting bigger and harder, thought Matt.

THIRTEEN

Chris showed up for practice, but he looked pale, thinner. Said he'd been up all night with a stomach virus. Coach Mac made him wear a red singlet along with Villanueva, who had a broken wrist after all. Injured, no contact. Chris ran routes, caught some passes from Brody's back-ups, held for Patel, and returned kickoffs. He didn't make eye contact with any of the seniors, and none of them talked to him. Matt stared hard at Chris several times, willing him to look back. He didn't want a conversation, he didn't know what he would say to the kid, but he wanted some kind of signal he was okay. Nothing.

It was a good practice, maybe because they focused so hard to make Chris invisible. Nobody mentioned him. Ramp made a lot of noise, clapping, yelling, reminding everyone it was only a few days to the opener. Matt wished he would shut up, but he was also glad one of them was acting like a captain. What's wrong with me? Talk to Monty about adjusting the dosage again? This was no time to be down.

School will start tomorrow, he thought, and I'll be back in that long, narrow tunnel of football, parties, and classes, moving straight ahead from game to game without having to think too much about anything else. I hope.

In the locker room after practice, Chris grabbed his street clothes and headed for the door without showering or changing.

"Missy Chrissie," yelled Ramp. "You going to the girls' locker room?"

Chris walked out without even turning around.

Pete said, "Leave him alone."

Ramp just grinned. "Jealous?" He grabbed his dick and waved it at Pete, then swaggered off to the showers.

Matt wondered what was going on in Pete's head. "Wassup?"

"Ramp's an asshole."

"There's a news flash." He punched Pete's shoulder. "You were right on."

"So why didn't you back me?"

"Why make a big deal when we need to be a team?"

Pete shook his head and walked away. That wasn't like him either.

Classes were okay. Coach Dorman, who was a guidance counselor, was teaching a health unit, Psychology of

Personality, that might be fun. Dad called Dorman "the touchy-feely coach," but Matt liked him. He seemed like someone who would listen. A lot of jocks and almost all the seniors on the football team were in the class. Dorman said he was going to give them one of the tests that NFL clubs used to evaluate potential draft picks.

Dad wasn't sure that was a good idea. "They could use those results against you," he said. They were eating dinner, and he was going over Matt's class schedule.

"Who would do that, Larry?" Asking a question like that was the closest Mom would get to disagreeing with him.

"Listen to the radio. Check the web. You can't be too careful these days."

"I listen to the radio and I'm careful," said Junie. He seemed happier now that he was back at his cafeteria job.

Dad ignored him. "Matt, you don't want to lose a scholarship because of some headshrinker's opinion."

"What do you think they'll find out?" said Matt. He knew he should leave it alone, but the old man was getting under his skin again.

"They'll find out Sarah likes you," said Junie. When everybody looked at him, he said, "She told me not to say anything."

"I'll bet she did," said Dad.

Mom said, "Matt, have you officially broken up with Amanda?"

"You think Sarah's gonna be angry?" said Junie.

"It's just what she wanted," said Dad. What was he pissed off about now? He stood up. "I got letters and e-mails from schools I never heard of." He stomped off to his den.

"She'll be glad you told me, Junie." Matt felt heat spread down from his stomach. Like to hook up with Sarah again. Be a way of cutting loose from Mandy without going through all the breakup drama. Once they'd been pushed together the spring of their junior year, a super couple whom everyone else wanted to hang around, he felt trapped with her in the social spiderweb.

"Matt?" said Mom. "You and Amanda?"

"What's the big deal?" He stood up.

"How you treat people is a very big deal."

"Got homework." That always worked.

FOURTEEN

Brody's parents had begun throwing a barbecue the night before opening game, right after the last pep rally, back in Freddy's day, when Brody and Matt were allowed to hang out if they helped with the cleanup. It was a major event this year because Matt and Brody were stars, and Rydek catered it. All the seniors on the varsity and their parents and girlfriends were invited, along with school and town big shots and the coaches. The cheerleaders and the Select Chorus were invited. Dad supervised the grills and Mr. Heinz handled the bar, making a big show of not handing drinks to the football players but winking and looking away when they grabbed beers out of the coolers. Tyrell didn't show. Mandy was fluttering around in her cheerleader queen mode, flirting with the older men and making a big deal of ignoring Matt.

You had to hand it to her, he thought. You'd never

know Mandy had been a clumsy fat girl in middle school. Then she had what Terri called "a makeover summer." The beginning of freshman year, nobody recognized Mandy at first. There was a rumor the new girl was a movie actress researching a role. When they figured it out, Mandy became an instant celebrity.

Sarah was helping Mom and Junie shake out the chips and arrange the corn and the salads. Matt was impressed by how smoothly Sarah had moved in. She was really nice with Junie. Mandy barely noticed him. Sarah made herself useful, got her hands wet and dirty. Mandy had always acted like someone who was born to be served.

Why am I comparing them? Mandy is probably the best-looking girl in school. She worked as hard at cheerleading as he did at football. Sarah's pretty good-looking and has a beautiful voice. Must have worked hard at that, too. He liked the way she jiggled under her tank top.

"Those jugs real?" asked Ramp.

"You'll never find out," said Matt.

"At least you're straight," said Ramp.

"What?"

Ramp lowered his voice. "You think Pete's gay?"

"Takes one to know one," said Brody. "You wanna lick my balls again, Ramp?"

"I'm serious," said Ramp. Matt thought he looked more sly than serious. "He's been acting queer lately."

"What's that mean?" snapped Matt.

"I always figured him the weak link," said Ramp.

"I know what you mean," said Brody. "He's sensitive, cares about people. He isn't a day-old dog turd like you."

Ramp took it because he had a plan, thought Matt. He could almost hear the machinery whirring in Ramp's brain. It reminded him of Dad switching gears in a conversation. Ramp said, "Pete talks to his girlfriend about Raider stuff."

"So?" said Matt.

"So you're a Raider all the way or you're not, that's all. What I meant by weak link."

"I know what you boys are doing." Mr. Koslo strolled up. "Deciding which one of you carries the Conference Cup in the town parade."

"The State Cup," said Brody. "This is our year."

"I love it." He slapped Brody on the shoulder. Mr. Koslo was a lawyer in the city who owned a lot of real estate around Nearmont. A few years ago, he raised a million dollars to renovate the field house and build a new weight room. Dad liked to be around him but behind his back said he was a crook who paid off politicians.

The mayor, Pastor Jim, and the police chief came up. They started talking Raider football, but Matt could see they wanted to hang out with Mr. Koslo. They didn't notice as Matt, Ramp, and Brody drifted back to the party.

Matt waited until Ramp went for a beer. "He's trying

to split us up, like Tyrell said."

"Where is Tyrell?" Brody looked around. "He was invited. You think that was his dope stash?"

"You believe that?" Matt stared at Brody until he shrugged. "He ever try to sell any dope? No. Ramp's spreading that to keep everybody off-balance, off his own ass."

"Wouldn't have thought he was that smart," said Brody.

Patel sauntered up and slipped each of them a beer. "You get busted, it didn't come from me."

"If they tortured me, Jay, I wouldn't say your name," said Brody. "By the way, what is it?"

Patel grinned and wandered over toward some girls waiting to be pushed into the pool.

The party didn't feel right to Matt. Something was off, like static on the radio, confusion in the huddle. Is it just me, he wondered, thinking about Chris and Tyrell, is it Mandy, making people notice her ignoring me? Or did people know that something had happened at camp? It looked all right, parents clustered at one end of the big yard, kids at another. Mrs. Heinz was down to her bikini and Corndog couldn't get close enough. Mr. Heinz and Dad were side by side at the grill, probably talking college football programs. They still had hopes for a package deal, Brody and Matt to the same school. Colorado had shown some interest in a package, but after the sex scandal broke

Dad stopped answering their e-mails. He thought that if Colorado was penalized postseason games and TV appearances, it could affect Matt's exposure for the NFL draft.

Matt turned on the mute when Dad started talking scholarship, about playing colleges off against each other, getting the best deal. Just get me out of here. His grades and SATs were good enough for a top school so long as he had a good season. He had the best shot of anyone in the Back Pack, but none of them ever seemed to begrudge his chances at big Bowl school. Brody and Tyrell would end up somewhere good. Pete might have to settle for a mid-major school, but football wasn't as important to him. Ramp's SATs and grades weren't good, but there were plenty of schools willing to take a chance on a mad-dog linebacker.

Why am I thinking about this?

Because you got to get out of here.

Matt watched Sarah and Junie giggling together as they served salad. Is she doing this just to get closer to me? I hardly know her and she's acting like a member of the family. He looked around again for Tyrell and spotted Mandy making sure everyone saw her flirting with Coach Dorman. Should I be feeling sorry for her trying so hard? I hardly feel anything for her.

"Ready to rock?" Freddy Heinz always looked a little down. Maybe the greatest athlete to come out of

Nearmont, all-state in football, basketball, and baseball. Nike was giving him shoes in middle school. Now look at him.

"Tomorrow's the day."

"Team looks good, even that retarded brother of mine." Freddy caught himself. "Sorry."

"'S okay." It wasn't, but hell, Freddy never meant anything mean.

"What happened with that big tight end, the phenom?"

"Who?" It took him an instant to realize Freddy was talking about Chris.

"He sure looked good in June."

"You saw him then?"

Freddy lowered his voice. "Coach Mac asked me and Brody to give him a little tryout, off the record, when the kid wanted to transfer. He didn't want to buy some other coach's problem unless it was worth it."

"Problem?"

"Got too friendly with another guy, know what I mean?"

"Not really," said Matt. "He tell you that?"

"Ramp told me. You think it's bullshit?"

"From Ramp?" Matt made a face.

"Know what you mean. So what happened? I didn't see him at practice last couple of days. He get hurt in camp?"

Matt looked at Freddy but couldn't read him. Did he know something? But Freddy wasn't tricky. Matt said, "Stomach virus."

Mr. Heinz called everybody over for toasts, and Matt never got the chance to find out if Freddy knew anything more.

FIFTEEN

Matt burst off the line at the snap, racing down the sideline toward the left cornerback, who stopped to brace himself for the collision. Mistake. Matt juked around him.

Put it in my hands, Brody.

He glanced over his shoulder for a snapshot of the field. Brody was still scrambling, pumping the ball, looking for a receiver. It was taking too long. His protection had collapsed around him in piles of red and white jerseys. Even Tyrell and Pete were on the ground. Ramp and Heller were covered.

I'm right here, Brody.

Searching. The word flickered in a corner of his mind the way it flickered on his cell phone screen when the signal faded. We're losing it, he thought. That hot wire between us has been disconnected.

He cut again and headed back to give Brody a target.

The crowd roared. Brody was down. A fumble. A white jersey, big and slow, was lumbering away. The crowd was jumping, screaming. West Closter was the weakest team in the conference, an easy opener for the Raiders. If we lose this one . . .

Matt took off after him. He could catch that three-hundred-pound wheezing freight train, but he might not be able to bring him down from behind. Cut him off, collide at an angle. It'll hurt, but it'll work. There was no way the ball carrier could avoid him and he didn't try. He let Matt slam into him and merely grunted, dragging him three yards before he fell on top of him. The officials had to untangle them, help them both up. Matt and the big West Closter kid looked at each other and nodded. Clean play—they had both done their jobs.

Matt waved the trainer away, but she pulled him off the field. He started to feel the pain in his ribs as West Closter pounded through for a touchdown but missed the point-after kick. The whistle for the half blew. It was 6–0.

Coach Mac was ranting in the locker room. They were quitters, whiners. They didn't deserve to be Raiders. They were lying down like sissies. Ramp picked it up, yelling at individuals, Heller, Pete, pussies, Hagen, Boda, gonna stuff tampons up your asses, Brody's just posing out there, Tyrell's sleepwalking, even the great Matt Rydek needs to step up. Ramp reamed himself for not hitting harder. The team stared at the grimy concrete floor of the visitors' locker room as the managers handed out orange slices and sports drinks. Student trainers rewrapped ankles and wrists, cleaned cuts and bruises, and sprayed on antiseptic. Matt peeked under his jersey. The skin over his ribs was red and swollen.

"We're flat," said Tyrell, sitting down next to him. "Nice tackle. Humongous mother."

"Didn't get his license plate." Matt smiled at his own joke.

Tyrell laughed.

Ramp loomed over them. "Why you laughing? You stoned?"

Tyrell cursed and started to stand up. Matt pulled him down. Ramp walked away.

"Someday, I'm gonna split that cracker's skull," said Tyrell.

"Get in line," said Pete. Blood was caked on the bridge of his nose. He looked at Matt. "You okay? I heard that hit thirty yards away."

"Nothing," said Matt. Try to use the pain to make me sharper, he thought.

Chris had dressed for the game but never played. He stayed in a corner of the locker room during halftime and sat alone with the scrubs at the end of the bench. Once Matt thought he was trying to catch his eye, but he looked away. Didn't want to lose concentration. Maybe after the game.

They weren't any better in the second half. If West Closter had a decent quarterback, we'd be way behind by now. Everything was a beat off, last season's team tightness gone. Brody had no confidence in his protection, so he was hurrying his throw or handing off too fast. Or keeping the ball and losing yards. Tyrell was getting pounded. Coach pulled him out to rest for two downs, and the offense totally stalled.

"Throw it to eighty," yelled Dad.

He had appeared midway through the third quarter, announcing himself in his bullhorn voice. "Let's go, Raiders. Let's go, Raiders." He was catering a fancy party but must have ducked out. Matt had hoped he wouldn't show. Dad could get especially obnoxious at away games. "Let's go, Raiders. West Closter sucks."

Shut up, thought Matt. He tried to avoid looking toward Dad but couldn't help himself. Dad had worked his way down to the first row of the grandstand behind the Raider bench. He was wearing a red and black Nearmont cap and a No. 80 jersey. Great. In another few minutes he'd be on the field behind the bench even though Coach Mac had gotten the conference to make a special rule banning unauthorized people from the field. That was aimed at Dad.

Time out. Villanueva was balancing a white plastic board on his wrist cast while Corndog drew Xs and Os. A new play they'd learned at camp.

Matt faked a cut at the snap, then streaked straight downfield. He heard a grunt and a laugh. Ramp must have put his helmet into the middle of a white jersey. He stopped at the whistle and turned. Tyrell had made a five-yard gain.

Back in the huddle, Brody was All-Brody again, acting sure of himself. He grinned at Matt. "Hunkies go long." An old joke from PeeWee.

This time, the cornerback didn't brace for the hit, he stayed up on his toes, so Matt bumped him out of the way and kicked into higher gear. He sensed the ball, it was on a string from Brody's hands to his, it was going to come down into the soft cup of his palms when he reached the end of its flight.

The "oooooh" of the crowd told him the ball was overhead and he was alone. Pain shot up his flank as he stretched for it. He felt it settle into his hands, drew it into his chest. He blotted out Dad's screaming. He needed to hear the breathing of the defenders.

The safety had the angle on him and was coming fast. Maybe I can juke past him, stay inside the white line, don't think about the hit, let it happen. Maybe twenty yards to go, got a chance, every foot counts, keep going, keep going. He thought he might have stepped over. Whistle.

He flipped the ball to the ref, who put it down twelve yards from the goal line.

Dad was on the sideline screaming, "You blind, he was in bounds, you work for West Closter?"

Tyrell and Pete slapped Matt's helmet. "Way to go." Everybody was trying to touch him. This was the best. We're back on track. If only the old fart would shut up.

Coach Mac sent a manager to Dad. The conference had also gotten together on harassing officials. There could be a penalty.

In the huddle, Brody said, "Same thing."

"They'll be expecting it," said Ramp.

"Just block," snapped Brody.

Matt crossed right, then streaked down the sideline again, taking the secondary with him. Ramp opened a hole for Pete, who ran straight down the middle, drawing in the corners. Tyrell took a handoff down to the two yard line. All-Brody sneaked over for the touchdown, and Patel kicked the extra point. They held on, 7–6, to the final whistle.

Dad was waiting at the bus as they climbed in for the ride back to school. "What's wrong with you?"

"We won."

He tried to push past, but Dad grabbed his arm. "You got to stand up for yourself with the zebras—they'll walk all over you. Don't be such a pussy. Good thing the Penn State guy didn't show."

Even Ramp looked away as he passed them. Matt pulled free and climbed on the bus. Brody made room for him on the backseat.

Coach Mac stormed up and down the aisle, yelling at everyone except Patel. He kept them sweating and stinking on the bus for a half hour in the West Closter parking lot, going over blown assignments and missed opportunities, while West Closter fans kicked the bus and cursed them. It was funny in a sick way.

Back at Nearmont, they showered and dressed in silence.

On the way out to their cars, Brody said, "You coming to Terri's tonight?"

He had forgotten about that. "I guess so."

"Wear a helmet. Mandy'll be there."

SIXTEEN

Sarah stuttered on the phone when he said he'd pick her up and they'd go to Terri's. He liked catching her off guard, poking a hole in her self-confidence. It made him feel a little bigger, more in control after the day's whippings. She said she hadn't been at the game, in fact she was still at work. She seemed hesitant to give him her address, said she'd meet him at the party, but he insisted on picking her up at home. He needed to get his way.

He thought he had gotten the address wrong when he pulled up at the ugly new condos near the highway on the edge of town. A square of concrete boxes with decks overlooking the parking lot. She was standing out front, looking good.

"The new house isn't ready, so we're renting here for a few months." She was talking fast as she climbed in. "It's a drag—everything's in storage. How was the game?"

"We sucked." He was surprised that he felt like telling her about it. "We weren't executing, we weren't working together."

"Sounds frustrating."

"We knew what to do but we couldn't do it."

"I know that feeling. Sometimes when the chorus isn't tight, you feel like a little kid again, everything's out of your control."

He felt comforted by her understanding, but alert, too. You don't want someone trying to get into your head, like Terri. Do you? Mandy never tried. That was a relief for a while. Then he figured she just didn't care. All-Mandy.

He liked the looks they got when they walked in. Shock and awe. Mandy scared people. No bitch rules Matt Rydek. He wondered if he was giving himself a pep talk.

Patel waved from across the room. A girl was hanging on him. He was a hero tonight. Wouldn't be running beers. Ramp lumbered by, did a comical double take at Sarah, then grinned and winked. Matt turned away and looked for Brody. Somebody handed them beers.

Pete slouched up. "Watch your ass. Mandy is volcanic."

"Vesuvius? Mount St. Helens?" Matt tried to remember more volcanoes.

"I'm serious. WYA. Hi, Sarah."

"Hi, Pete." She took Matt's arm and steered him into the thick of the party. Clumps of kids peeled away to let them through to Mandy, the queen on a couch, snuggling up to a guy who had graduated a few years ago. College guy.

Brody was sitting nearby with Terri. How'd they get so tight? Everybody looked a little wasted already. Brody gave him a little head shake. Take off.

Too late.

"Look who dragged the cat in." Mandy sat up. "You've got some fucking nerve, Matt, showing up with that fag hag."

Even if he wanted to split now, he couldn't, kids pressing in all around them. Hard to breathe. What was he trying to prove?

The college guy piped up. "Maybe you should just leave, pal." But he didn't stand up. No threat there.

"Maybe you should just kiss my ass, pal."

The college boy started to untangle himself from Mandy, but she held on to him. She knew Matt could take him.

"Just get the fuck out," Mandy said. "Take that Wal-Mart slut with you. Did you do her mother, too?"

"You loser," snarled Sarah. He could feel her body vibrating against his. "All that liposuction and you still can't hold on to your man."

"Whore!" Mandy launched herself off the couch,

right at Sarah, her red-tipped fingernails clawing the air.

Sarah froze. He heard her gasp.

Instinct and training clicked in. He spun Sarah out of the way, dropped a shoulder, and let Mandy slam into it. There was a *thunk* and a moan. He reached out to grab her as she fell, a mistake, and the red claws raked his cheek. He let go, and she slumped to the floor, crying and sucking air. The party swarmed around her.

Ramp was laughing. "Nice block, Rydek." He raised his hand for a high five. Matt ducked under it and pulled Sarah through the crowd and out of the house.

SEVENTEEN

They drove around for a while, not talking, listening to a new CD without hearing it. They ended up three towns away at a diner packed with middle-aged couples who must have just come from a nearby cineplex. Nobody here we'd know, he thought.

Sarah was pale, her eyes red rimmed. She pushed her French fries around her plate with her fork.

"You okay?"

He had to say it twice before she said, "I'm really sorry."

"For what?"

"I guess I had something to prove. Stupid."

"I took you there."

She looked up. "We should put peroxide or something on your face."

"Wouldn't want to get cat scratch fever." It just came out. Funny line.

It got a smile out of her. Some of the color came back into her face. "It was so embarrassing."

"She should be embarrassed," said Matt. "She acted like a jerk."

Sarah reached across the table to touch his cheek.

The good warmth spread down from his belly. "So, you gonna take me to the emergency room?"

Her tinkly laugh was back. "I was thinking of intensive care."

They drove back to the condo. Her mother was out of town working, she said. It was a small, neat apartment. It looked like a motel suite. A cat saw Matt and scurried away. Sarah led him into the bathroom, sat him down on the toilet lid, and found peroxide and gauze pads in the cabinet.

There was a splash of pain, then they were kissing, pulling at each other's clothes. He palmed a condom before his pants came down.

He didn't remember how they got to her bedroom. They swept stuffed animals off her bed.

She wasn't shy, didn't wait for him to make the first moves, like Mandy. She seemed as fierce and hungry as he was. It excited and scared him, her hands squeezing and tugging all over his body. He had to concentrate to match her energy. Some part of him wanted to hold back, to stay on guard as their bodies slipped over each other on flimsy layers of sweat.

"Matt!" Her hand was on the bruise over his ribs. He bit his lip. The pain chewed up his side. "That must hurt."

"It's nothing."

"I've got something." She was gone.

He took a deep breath. Mistake. A sledgehammer banged his ribs.

She was back with a small plastic jar. "Old family remedy. Just relax."

He tried to relax. When was the last time he totally relaxed with a girl? A soft hand glided over the bruise; the cream stung a little at first, then heat seeped into his skin. He let himself sink into the bed.

"Better?"

"Better."

"I want to make you feel good, Matt." She kissed him.

"You do."

"I mean really. Not just, you know."

He felt the heat off her body like a dry bath. He stroked her smooth soft cheek. They took in each other's breaths. It was very peaceful. He could feel all thoughts drain out of his mind.

"Matt? I lied to you," she said. He couldn't see her features clearly in the bedroom. "I live here with my mom. She's a night inventory manager for Wal-Mart. I work there, too. My dad walked out on us after his big birthday party. We had to sell the house."

"Must be tough."

"Everybody's got problems." She spread more cream on the bruise. The pain faded. "Your dad's a piece of work, too."

"No kidding." He felt safe here with her.

"You stand up to him. I love how you protect your brother."

Safe but a little scared, too. Can she see inside me? "Junie's a good kid."

"Is Junie his real name?"

"Junior. He was named after Dad, but I think Dad's sorry now."

"That's so sad. Everything's on you." Her other hand stroked his face. "All that pressure and you're still so strong, so steady. Most people would be druggies."

He laughed at that. "If you don't call steroids and Vicodin drugs. For starters." Why was he telling her this?

"Isn't that dangerous, the steroids?"

"Not if you're careful. I got somebody helping me, knows what he's doing. Steroids are healing drugs. I can work out harder and repair muscle faster." He'd never talked so freely to a girl before. It felt good. "It's not like I'm doing coke or crank. These are prescription drugs."

"What about side effects?"

"You got to pay the price if you want to make it."

"Make it?"

"Division One. Maybe the pros." Definitely the pros, but you don't want to jinx it.

"Is that what you want to be, a pro football player?"

"Sound crazy to you?"

"No. I wanted to sing at the Metropolitan Opera."

"Wanted?" This felt so easy, so warm. Too easy, too warm. WYA. He didn't feel sexy. He felt . . . happy.

"I had to stop taking lessons after Dad split. It's very expensive. There's a lot of travel to workshops and teachers, voice, diction, repertoire. And you're not even sure until you're in your thirties that you have a chance."

"That's when most football players hang it up."

She laughed. "I'll take over the spotlight when you're finished with it."

"You have a beautiful voice."

"Thank you." She started rubbing in cream again.

He pushed the jar away and pulled her close.

Something was wrong. He wasn't hard.

Never happened before. Was it the Vics? After the game, he'd popped one, another with a beer before he drove to Sarah's. Another beer at Terri's. Was that enough to lose a woodie? Vics and brew don't mix.

"Sorry, I—"

"It happens."

"Not to me."

"Sometimes it happens"—she sounded dreamy—"when you're with someone you really want. Someone you really care about."

Never happened with Mandy, even after a game,

floating on beer and Vics. In bed, he and Mandy shared the zone. They knew each other's moves.

Sarah held him for a while. He felt small, childish. Like she was his mom. When she went to the bathroom, he pulled on his underpants. He needed to be covered.

"You want something? Beer, wine. There's Diet Coke, orange juice." She was smiling as if it were no big deal, he thought. It was a big deal. Was she trying to make him feel better because she felt sorry for him? "Ice cream?"

"I'm sorry." He felt ashamed. His father's face, twisted with anger at Junie, popped into his head, then Sarah comforting Junie. She's good with boys who aren't normal.

"For what?"

"You know."

But she didn't. Or pretended she didn't. Finally, as if remembering something from long ago, she said, "Oh, that. You're tired and all beat up. You're not a machine."

"I should go."

"Why?"

"It's late." He had no idea of the time.

"We could watch some DVDs." She didn't want him to leave even though he couldn't execute. Why? So she'd have something on him? "Let me put more salve on the bruise."

He needed to get out of here. Now. He followed the trail of clothes they had dropped, dressing piece by piece in different rooms. Back in the bathroom, he popped another Vicodin and washed it down with water cupped in his hand.

She followed him in. "Was it something I did?" She sounded desperate. That scared him. "Please, let me—"

"Gotta go." He didn't look at her as he hurried out.

He felt better outside. There was just enough of a breeze to dry the sweat. He was dizzy. He bumped his head getting into the Jeep.

He thought about getting on the highway and letting the traffic take him somewhere, anywhere, but he was having trouble focusing on the road ahead. He didn't want to go home. Nowhere to go. Too much to think about.

A siren sliced into his brain. Flashing red and white lights grew into a poisonous flower in his rearview mirror. He pulled over.

"Matt?" The cop poked his head through the open window. "You're all over the road. Been drinking?"

"Pain pills."

"Been there." Big guy, thick neck. He had played. "Some shot you took today."

"You at the game?"

"Never miss 'em. You live on Harrington, right? Can you follow me? I'll get you home."

"Thanks." Some part of him wanted to say, Bust me.

He had to concentrate to stay in his lane. A memory popped up, Dad waking him up to show him off to the poker game in the rec room. Mr. Heinz and the mayor were there. They were all smoking cigars. He had scored three touchdowns in the PeeWee championship game that day. Dad gave him a cigar. They all laughed as he started to get sick on the second puff.

He tasted the vomit again as he followed the cop home.

EIGHTEEN

On Sunday, the e-mails starting piling up from screen names he didn't recognize. He never got that many messages except from the football coaches and managers, mostly schedules and reminders and pep talks. He was no writer, so he never encouraged e-pals. He preferred quick cell phone calls or even text messages. But by the time he checked, late on a long, sluggish Sunday, there were at least two dozen unopened messages. The sight of them drained what little energy was starting to seep back from protein shakes and amphetamines. He hadn't felt like eating and his ribs ached. The Vics were making him nauseous.

Dad had left early for a wedding. After a while, Mom and Junie had given up trying to drag him out of bed. They were going to church and then to a town fair. Junie loved fairs. But there was no way Matt was going to be around people today.

Brody had called to invite him over to watch the NFL games on his monster plasma screen, but Matt said he had to go with Mom and Junie. Brody forgot lies, too. The thought of Mrs. Heinz in her bikini made him remember last night. What happened? Am I losing it? I'm not gay. Was it the steroids? Who could you ask about that? Monty? Feel weird.

What did Sarah really think about a guy who couldn't get it up? Mandy called her a fag hag. Maybe that's why she likes me.

He'd pushed her out of his mind and slapped the mattress until Romo understood she was welcome to jump onto the bed. They snuggled for a while, then went downstairs to cuddle on the couch and watch the games. These guys are so huge, Matt thought, so ripped and fast, so willing to sacrifice their bodies on every play. Imagine the drugs they were taking. What do I have to do to get to the NFL? Switch to cornerback? Gain fifty pounds?

After the Giants game, he'd caught the back end of a Yankee doubleheader. He loved Jeter. Class and talent and guts. And a real captain and role model. Didn't have to call meetings and yell at guys, he thought, just showed them how to act by example. Baseball was my game, too, until the football trophies started coming in. Man, I loved the outfield, all alone until suddenly you are the only one between the ball and an extra-base hit. Some great catches sophomore year on the JV, hitting a ton. They brought me up to the varsity for the final two games of the season. Got hot.

But Dad and Coach Mac said he had to make a choice. The lifting programs for baseball and football were different, and spring football practice was too important to miss. This is the age of specialization, said Coach Mac. You've got to pay the price, Matt. Dad thought his chances for a full ride in Division One were better in football than baseball. More scholarships available. More TV exposure. And pro baseball was turning Latino—you'll be up against all those Dominicans willing to work for the minimum to escape their island. It was another year or so before Matt began wondering if Dad just didn't want him to succeed in baseball because he didn't make it.

He had wanted to play baseball, but he caved. He let Coach Mac and Dad make the decision for him. The cocaptaincy was part of the deal to tie him up, he later thought. It was announced at spring practice junior year, and it made him feel responsible to the football team. He never really wanted to be a captain, to be in charge of other people, to have to worry about them. Not his thing. Just wanted to look out for himself and his friends. When it was announced, some of the guys said they were glad they could go to him instead of Ramp, and that made him feel better.

He still missed baseball. Something so clean and true about baseball. You weren't so dependent on guys you didn't trust to watch your back.

When he heard Mom and Junie pull into the garage, he went up to his room and closed the door. Poor Romo whined and tried to scratch her way in, but with her inside it would be impossible to keep Junie out. Matt wasn't up for his brother's energy, for the minute-by-retarded-minute replay of his day. He felt ashamed for thinking that.

Then the anonymous e-mails drove everything else out of his mind.

"Think you can get away with it?"

"Dream on, asshole."

"No wat u did."

"U suck shit."

"WYA."

He deleted the rest without opening them. He didn't recognize any of the addresses, but they were probably from Mandy's friends. He knew that crap goes away after a while if you don't respond, don't let them think they're getting to you. But what if it's about Chris? Creepy seeing him sitting on the bench like a ghost. I should try to talk to him at school tomorrow. About what? Matt was sweating.

He didn't want to think about it. He let Junie into the room and listened to the endless play-by-play of church and the town fair. He let it wash out his head. Another Vic kept him smiling through dinner.

Dad wanted to talk to him afterward. Grabbed his

arm and pulled him into the den. Closed the door. Pushed him into a wooden chair.

"What's going on?"

"About what?"

"Don't play with me, Matt." He had the no-expression mask on and his eyes were slits.

What did Dad know? The e-mails, Mandy, Sarah, Chris? The world was dropping a box over his head. Hard to breathe. Maybe I should just spill it all out before I smother and die.

Stay cool. Can't go on like this.

"Can't go on like this." Did Dad say that, or me? "Not if you still plan on Division One."

"Just the first game." What are we talking about? Matt thought.

"Do you want to go D-One?" His face was an inch away, too close to see clearly, but the stink of red wine made Matt gag. "DO YOU?"

He breathed. "Yeah."

Dad pulled back, stared at him, then suddenly collapsed back into his recliner. "Oh, man." He rubbed his eyes with the heels of his hands. "You don't want to end up like me, Matt, working all the goddamn time. I want you to have a life, get somewhere."

Matt felt uncomfortable. Where's he going with this?

"You gonna tell me what's going on?" He lowered his voice. "Maybe I can help."

Matt remembered a documentary about kids who walked across fields in Cambodia looking for unexploded mines. Most dangerous job in the world. One misstep, *kaboom*. Here goes. "What do you think I should do?"

"Execution, it's all about execution." Dad sat up, smiling. He loved to lecture. "Brody's not looking for you fast enough, he's thinking about himself. He's trying to pile up personal stats, so he's scrambling all the time. I've talked to his dad, friggin' Wall Street blowhard." Dad was cranked. "Brody should stay in the pocket until he can hit you. Hand off to the little monkey once in a while, even to Pete, slow as he is, as a change of pace. Too bad that new kid didn't work out. What's his problem?"

"Chris Marin?" He felt a chill saying his name.

"Wasn't he supposed to start?"

"Got sick."

"Or scared." Dad smirked. "Be surprised how many guys can't take the heat, fold in the clutch. They get sick, get hurt, drive into a tree just because they can't pay the price." He reached out to grab Matt's shoulder. Matt tried not to flinch, almost succeeded. Dad didn't notice. "I know you'll do what you need to do. Make us all proud. Glad we had a chance to talk."

"Yeah," said Matt. He nodded as Dad patted his butt and steered him out of the den. Didn't step on the mine. Maybe I will someday.

NINETEEN

School seemed different, the halls higher, wider, an echo chamber of jumbled sound. Usually he felt big in the halls, enjoying the way kids smiled up at him or looked away. Depending on his mood, he'd let his shoulders clear the way, bumping punks and jerk-offs and other jocks, or he'd twist and turn like a broken-field runner to avoid contact with smaller guys and girls. He liked playing humble hero. It made him feel even bigger, more in control.

He never bullied kids in school, like Ramp and his pals did. Once he even stopped a trash canning in the cafeteria, some football players having fun with a violin nerd. Got a lot of props from nonjocks for that. They never knew he did it because he thought it would be bad for the team. He had always felt he could do anything he wanted in the hall, but now suddenly he felt smaller, more prey than hunter. Even the desks seemed bigger. Usually he had to angle himself into a tight fit. Today he had room, even for his long legs.

Modern American lit, French, biology, global economics rolled past. He heard nothing. In the fall semester, nobody called on football players unless they raised their hands. Pay the price in the spring.

He spotted Sarah before she saw him, in the cafeteria. He made sure he was looking the other way when she called, "Matt!" She was standing with the tall fat kid who sang in Select Chorus with her. Matt had been in a few classes with him, smart kid, nice enough, but fruity, not someone you talked to when other players were around.

Matt let the crowd take him around the corner and outside. He'd grab something at a food stand or skip lunch. What was there to say to her? What could she want to talk to him about?

He pulled his cap down, didn't look around much, got through the day. At practice, Pete said, "Trainer said Chris had a doctor's excuse for today, a doctor in the city."

Practice was lifeless. The coaches were screaming. Ramp was running around pulling face masks and banging shoulder pads. But they couldn't start the engine. Coach Mac blew the whistle early and signaled Matt to follow him into his office. The froggy reporter was standing outside the door.

"I'm busy right now," Coach Mac told him. He closed

the door and sagged into his desk chair. He pointed Matt to the couch. "That kid's a pest. Always looking for dirt. Must be practicing for the media. How the ribs feel?"

"Fine."

"You're tough. Wish they were all as steady as you, Matt. So. We got a problem." On the pause, Matt held his breath. "On offense." Coach's eyes widened at Matt's exhalation. Not too cool. What does he know? "We can't let them double-team you. Tyrell's not enough. This Marin kid could make the difference, but I hate to say it, he needs a heart transplant. I don't think he's as sick as he says, and if he misses any more games and practices, it'll be too late. Got to stiffen him up. Can I count on you?"

"What do you want me to do?"

"Talk to him. You're the captain."

"Why me?" Did Coach know about Chris and Ramp?

"I think he'll listen to you. Calm him down. He needs to know how important this season is to the school, the town, how he can be part of a championship. How he has to put the team ahead of himself. I think his mother's part of the problem. No dad around, she's babying him. He's got to learn that a man does what it takes, that to get to the future you've got to get past the past. You understand what I'm saying?"

"I'll talk to him at practice tomorrow."

"No practice tomorrow for you. Mr. Koslo is sending a car to pick you and Chris up after eighth period."

"Skip practice?"

"You'll be his guests at Yankee Stadium."

"A Yankee game?" Matt felt confused.

Coach Mac rolled his eyes. "You think I'd let you skip practice for a rap concert?"

"Why?"

"Give you and Mr. Koslo a chance to make Chris feel more comfortable here, get past any issues." Coach stood up. "Need a permission slip from your parents. By the way, the Penn State scout told me he was impressed how you stopped that big horse."

"Thought he didn't show."

"Who told you that?" The phone rang. Coach picked it up and said, "Right with you," and put a hand over the mouthpiece. "See the trainer before you go. Maybe she should wrap your ribs."

Coach knows something, thought Matt. Doesn't want me to know how much. Maybe we can get past all this.

The reporter was still at the door when Matt came out of Coach Mac's office. He handed Matt a business card. Cool. A high school kid with a business card. "I'd like to interview you. Is there dissension on the team?"

"Gotta go now." He kept moving.

"Something happen at camp? We could do this by e-mail."

He waited until he turned the corner before he trash canned the card.

Something happen at camp? Word's out. But how much? Enough for the big booster to take us to a Yankee game.

The parking lot was nearly empty by the time he was done and dressed. The trainers had held a conference over his ribs, surprised at how the bruises had faded. He said he'd put something on it but didn't go into details. They told him to rub on some more and gave him some tape and gauze pads to cover it. He was thinking he'd never see any more of that magic stuff when he spotted Sarah's car parked next to his. She was standing at his door. No escape.

"Hi." Like nothing happened. Well, nothing happened.

"Hi."

"You forgot this." She handed him a plastic bottle of the cream. "It really works, doesn't it?"

"Trainers thought so."

"Your side feels better?"

"Yeah."

"So, uh, there's going to be a concert next week at the county center, and the Select Chorus is performing. Can I save you a ticket?"

"I don't know. Extra practices."

"Well, I sent you an e-mail yesterday, so if you—"

"Didn't see it. I deleted everything."

"You've been getting them, too?" When he nodded,

she said, "It's a campaign. Amanda and the coven. Pretty gross."

"Yeah. I better get going." Some part of him wanted to stay with her, let her rub more cream on his ribs. He couldn't look her in the eye. She knew too much about him.

"Me, too. Gotta buy some touch-up for my car."

"What happened?"

"Come look."

The gouges on the driver's door of the Jetta were deep. Someone had carved an 80.

"Sorry." Why did I say that? he thought. I didn't do it.

"If you don't mind," she said, "I might just leave it."

"Why would you leave it?"

She laughed as she opened her door. "Tell you next time."

TWENTY

Chris said, "Thought they'd send at least a stretch Hummer for you, Matt."

The driver was holding open the door of a black limousine. Kids pouring out of school slowed to watch them climb in. Matt sank into the leather seat and relaxed. He'd been uptight for twenty-four hours wondering how he was going to deal with the kid, and suddenly it looked okay. Chris seemed friendly enough; even some of his old cocky self was back. Once they started toward the city, he began opening the limo's cabinets, shelves with neatly stacked magazines and newspapers, CDs and videocassettes, a minibar with candy, nuts, soda, beer, and little bottles of wine and hard booze.

"Mr. Koslo says help yourself." The driver's voice came over the intercom from the other side of the glass partition. "But no alcohol."

"He knows me," said Matt. That got a grin out of Chris. Matt pulled out a bottled water. Chris took a can of soda. "Yankee fan?"

"Mets," said Chris. "When we lived in the city, my dad took me to Shea all the time. He knew Mike Piazza. I wore his jersey. Got an autographed bat."

The kid was talking too fast and didn't make eye contact. He looked out the window. The limo turned onto the Palisades Parkway. The Hudson River glistened below them. It always surprised Matt how close New York was to Nearmont. The city had always scared him a little, even when he went in on a Friday night with the Back Pack to cruise downtown for girls. You could be free in the city, get lost in the city.

"So, who's this dude?" Chris waved his soda can around the limo.

"Mr. Koslo? You know the garden apartments in Ridgedale? The Knickerbocker Mall? He owns them. He played on the team back in like the seventies." He knew more but that was enough. Rydek Catering had worked some of Koslo Real Estate's parties, and Dad had steamed over being treated like help by a guy who was third string when he was a starter. "Mr. Koslo's good for summer jobs."

"If I'm still around." Now the kid was staring at the river, but Matt could tell he wanted to talk. Do I? About what? That night? Right. But Coach gave me a job to do.

"You'll be around. Coach likes you." He waited for Chris to turn his head. "But you got to show up at practice. You got to get past the past."

"What?"

"To get to the future you got to get past the past."

"Whatever you say." He went back to the river. His voice was dull. "My mom doesn't like the area. We might go back to the city. Or out west."

"That cool with you?"

"She's been having a hard time since my dad died."

"Sorry about that." He kept his voice neutral. If Chris wanted to lie about his dad, that was his business.

"Iraq." He was suddenly glaring at Matt, as if daring him to challenge him.

"That was his Army duffel bag." Matt's stomach tightened. Have I gone too far? He brought that duffel to camp. Matt could see Yankee Stadium up ahead.

"Yeah." Chris nodded. The glare softened. Then he looked away. "Coach really likes me?"

"They were designing a new offense around you. Never did that for me."

"Don't know if I can play yet. Still weak. Stomach is all fucked up."

"Virus, right?"

"Saw a doctor in the city. Gave me some pills to help me chill. You ever do that?"

Matt laughed. "Ups, downs, whatever." He decided to

risk a minefield walk. "You ever take anything to, like, build muscle?"

"Steroids? Some of the guys at Central were juicing. I was going to check it out this year, but . . ." He shrugged. "You?"

Matt nodded. "Something we could talk about if you decide to commit yourself to the program." He felt like a salesman. A little sleazy, but it was his assignment. "Need you, man. Could be a helluva season. Have some fun. It's a great school for ballplayers. Town really supports the team. Girls."

"You do pretty good in that department." Chris grinned. "That cheerleader is some fox. Best-looking girl in school, I think. I saw her at your locker today."

Mandy still had his combination. Forgot to change it. What was in there? Mostly books. Most of his stuff was in his football locker in the field house. Thinking about having to deal with Chris had cleared out his mind for anything else. Hadn't checked e-mail last night.

"What was she was doing?"

"She had her posse around her."

"Ex-girlfriend."

"Uh-oh. Maybe she planted a bomb in there."

"Could be." He felt like talking. He thought of Sarah. Proud to wear No. 80 on her car door. "She was pissed I hooked up with somebody else while she was gone."

"Use 'em and lose 'em, I say."

The limo was pulling up to the stadium's VIP entrance. "You meet anybody you like yet?"

"Still looking around."

"Make the starting team and they'll be looking for you."

The driver gave them tickets, and ushers escorted them to box seats right behind the visitors' dugout. They could see the Yankee bench across the field. Players were kidding around, scratching themselves, finding their bats, and running out to hit. Pitchers were casually shagging flies in the outfield and talking to each other. A coach was slapping grounders at the infielders. The loudspeakers blared, and an elevated subway train rumbled just outside the ballpark.

Matt felt himself slipping sweetly into his old baseball dreams, imagining himself running across the green outfield where Babe Ruth, Joe DiMaggio, Mickey Mantle, and Reggie Jackson once ran. He'd seen them all on ESPN Classic. Seen himself.

"Used to play baseball," he said. "Outfield."

"Me, too." Chris high-fived him. "Loved the game. Coach gave me a hard time, always on my case. Tried to change my swing."

"At Bergen Central?" When the kid nodded, he asked, "That why you left?"

"Good a reason as any," Chris snapped. He softened his voice. "So you really think we have a shot this season?"

"If we can get tight as a team," said Matt.

"Get past the past." It sounded sarcastic.

Ignore the attitude. "Yeah. Those guys pay the price, too." They watched Jeter and A-Rod scamper in and out of the batting cage, lining ropes into the outfield. I'd like to be doing that, Matt thought. Had he made the wrong choice? About what? Was he really making the choices?

"Don't get any ideas now—you're football players." Coach Dorman slipped into a seat behind them. "You get the limo and I get the bus and subway. That's the way it goes. C'mon—Mr. Koslo wants to say hello. He's not staying for the game."

TWENTY-ONE

The skybox was bigger than Sarah's living room. It was filling up with men and women dressed for the office, everybody just a little sweaty and tired. He'd been to enough Rydek Catering gigs to spot a business party. Mr. Koslo moved around, shaking hands, making sure everybody had drinks. Are we business, too? At buffet tables, servers were placing slices of roast beef and turkey, scoops of pasta and salad, on white china plates. Pretty fancy, but the view of the field was so high and angled, you might as well watch one of the four TVs.

"Matt! Lookin' good." Mr. Koslo clapped his shoulder. "And this must be Chris." He steered them to the buffet table. "You boys get yourselves something to eat. I've got to say hello to a few people—then we can talk."

Chris snatched a glass of wine off a passing tray and poured it into a water glass. Smooth move. He grinned when he saw Matt watching him. Matt thought of doing it, too, but didn't want to look like a copycat. He popped a Vicodin and filled his plate. He found an empty seat in the front row of the skybox looking down on the field. The grounds crew was raking the infield.

"I could get used to this." Dorman sat down with a loaded plate. He lowered his voice. "How's the kid doing?"

"Says he's okay." He followed Dorman's line of sight across the room. Chris was listening to Mr. Koslo, who was steering him out of the skybox. Where were they going?

"Needy boy, has issues," said Dorman. "We have to reach out, make him feel secure."

"What kind of issues?" Matt was surprised to hear himself. He usually avoided getting into this kind of stuff.

"I shouldn't be telling you this, but since his father went away, his mother's been in real bad shape." They stood for the national anthem. Matt had to lean close to hear Dorman. Went away? Did that mean he wasn't dead? Didn't Ramp say something about being in prison? "She's dumping her fears and anger on Chris. She's trying to convince him that something bad happened to him in training camp.

"She wants to stick it to the world right now, and Nearmont High's the easiest target. Poor Chris is torn between loyalty to his mom and loyalty to the team. He feels pulled in both directions. We've got to let him know he's part of the team and we're behind him."

Behind him. The words triggered an image that almost made Matt gag.

Mr. Koslo and Chris came back into the skybox and walked over to Matt. Dorman slipped away as they sat down.

"You know," said Mr. Koslo, waving his wineglass around the skybox, "I'd trade all this in a New York minute to be back in a uni with you guys. Best time in my life." He laughed. "Didn't know it then, of course, who does? Wanted to get out of high school into real life. But high school is as real as it gets. I wouldn't have all this if I hadn't learned to take it and dish it out when I was a Raider. They still do swirlies?"

"Not in a while," said Matt.

"Swirlies?" said Chris.

"On Raider Pride Night they used to push your face in a toilet bowl," said Mr. Koslo, laughing himself into a coughing fit. "If they thought you needed it, there'd be more than water in the bowl, get my drift." He winked.

Mr. Koslo put his hand on Chris's shoulder. Matt thought of Romo being petted. "First year's tough—gotta prove yourself, especially to yourself. But then you find out who you are, and they can never take that away from you." He pushed himself up on Chris's shoulder. "My knees never got over those years. Gotta go downtown.

Stay as long as you like, fellas, enjoy. Coach Dorman'll get the driver when you're ready to go." He gave them each a business card. "Call me anytime. Next summer maybe we can find some honest work for you guys."

Chris rolled his eyes as Mr. Koslo walked away. "Is he for real?"

Matt wasn't sure, but he nodded.

It was Dorman's suggestion that they go back downstairs to watch the game. Maybe snag a foul. Chris swiped another wine on the way out of the skybox.

Matt got his head into the game, a pitchers' battle for a few innings. The Indians loaded the bases, but A-Rod ended their rally with a diving catch in foul territory, headfirst into the visitors' dugout in front of them. Dorman got all excited. "That's what it's all about—you can't think about getting hurt, you got to be ready to sacrifice to win."

"But what if he busted his head open?" said Chris. "Broke a shoulder for a lousy foul pop."

Dorman laughed. "I know you're yanking my chain. No football player thinks like that."

The Indians never recovered, and the Yanks were 8–1 when Dorman reminded them it was a school night. He called the driver on his cell.

Dorman did most of the talking on the way home. "Defense is where it's at these days, all sports, all levels. Pitching is defense. In football, you can score on defense, which makes defense the new offense. Understand? I see Matt an all-pro cornerback, scoring touchdowns on interceptions. Chris, middle linebacker could be your NFL ticket, you score after you strip the ball."

Chris nodded mechanically. Matt turned on the mute until the driver pulled into the park-and-ride off the highway where Dorman had left his car. As soon as the coach was out of the limo, Chris opened the minibar and grabbed three little bottles. He flipped one to Matt.

"You buy that defense shit?" Chris cracked a bottle open and sucked it right down.

"Whatever it takes." Matt was tired.

"What does that mean?" He cracked the second bottle.

Matt wondered if he was supposed to stop him from drinking it. "Look, Chris, you got to get past the past, pay the price. You want to play?"

"You don't understand."

Should I say I do, that I know about your crazy mother, that you've got to make a choice if you don't want to wreck the team? Suck it up. We all do.

"We all have problems."

"What's yours?" said Chris. It sounded more like a question than a challenge.

"Got all night?"

That seemed to satisfy him. "You trust Koslo?"

"What'd he want?"

Chris's face was twisted. "I can't tell you."

The limo pulled up in front of a small house on a quiet old street. Chris drained the second bottle and dropped it on the floor. He got out without saying good night.

Matt drank his little bottle.

TWENTY-TWO

The pink star glued to the outside of his hall locker didn't register until he opened the locker. Taped to the inside of the door over his class and football schedules was a computer printout of a porn picture, a muscular young guy naked except for a football helmet. He was grinning and cradling himself, just the way Ramp and the linemen had on Raider Pride Night. A cartoon balloon drawn over his head in purple lipstick contained the words "Yo, 80, this make you hard?"

Matt slammed the locker shut and scratched off as much of the pink star as he could. What was left looked like shaving nicks.

It didn't seem like something Mandy would do, he thought. As if I really know her. But Chris said he saw her at the locker yesterday. Matt imagined finding Mandy and jamming the bitch into his locker, banging it shut on her red-painted claws. He took a long breath and swallowed the rage back, the way Monty had taught him. Then he pushed it into a far corner of his mind.

He could still do that.

He could always do that. Focus. Aim a steady eye on the goal ahead.

It got him through the day, into practice.

Ramp said, "You and Missy Chrissie have a good night together?"

Matt snapped, "Get your head out of your ass and into the game."

Ramp blinked.

Chris didn't show up at practice, and Matt forgot about him after the first hit. He had a great practice. When a JV cornerback on the scout team tried to force Matt out of bounds after a nice over-the-shoulder catch, he leveled him. The kid hadn't gone for a hard-ass tackle, more like a sheepdog herding a lamb, but Matt turned in on him and rammed a shoulder into his breastbone. *Crunch.* The kid went down groaning, and Matt raced down the sideline to the end zone. That woke up the team. Corndog gave him a fist. On the next play, Ramp decked Hagen, making a hole for Tyrell. Everybody was fired up. Matt felt better. Focus. It's always been the answer. Don't let anybody distract you. He was sorry to hear the whistle.

He slapped Tyrell's pads. "Great practice."

Tyrell just looked at him and walked away. That wasn't like him. Don't think about it.

At dinner, Dad said, "So did Koslo deliver?"

"What?"

"The Marin deal. Why you went to the stadium."

Why does he always know more than I do? "Why?"

Dad smirked. "Blowhard said he was going to help the kid with college if he stayed on the team. Know anything about it?"

So that was what Chris couldn't tell me. Koslo must have offered him a scholarship to keep quiet about Raider Pride Night and sworn him to secrecy about it. Not just to stay on the team. Wouldn't Dad love to hear the real story.

Matt shrugged. "Dunno."

Dad waited until Junie was busy feeding Romo from his plate. He lowered his voice. "Anything to what the kid's mother says?"

"About what?" Sometimes you can feel so smart acting dumb.

"About something happening to him in camp?"

"Like what?"

"I'm asking you." He was annoyed. "Can't you give me a straight answer?"

"Ask a straight question."

Junie piped up. "How can a question be straight?"

"Don't feed that dog off your plate," said Dad.

Junie looked confused.

"Leave him alone," said Matt.

"Don't you talk to me in that tone," said Dad.

What are you going to do about it? He tasted the words, salty and crunchy, but didn't let them out of his mouth.

Mom said, "Does the Marin boy date?"

"Nobody 'dates,'" said Matt.

"Felice Miller heard a rumor about him getting into trouble at Bergen Central with another boy."

Lisa's mom, thought Matt. Had Pete told Lisa about camp? They'd been going out since eighth grade. Dating. "Where'd she hear that?"

"Vikki Heinz."

Who heard it from Freddy. Who heard it from Ramp.

"Man," said Dad. "Some people have too much time on their hands." He hated it when people knew things he didn't know. He looked at his watch. "Homework, mister. Michigan and Notre Dame are going to want to see midterm grades. Make sure you don't slack off during the season."

"Notre Dame?" said Mom. "Don't you have to be Irish Catholic?"

Dad put her down with a snorting laugh. "You can be a Black Hebe if you're Heisman material." He fired a forefinger at Matt. "Upstairs."

He was glad to escape.

He never would have opened the e-mail if he hadn't

liked the idea of a recruiting letter slipping past Dad. The e-mail was from COACHRIGHT69.

A picture came right up of Chris and Matt screwing.

The heads didn't fit the bodies, which were doing it doggie style. Matt was on top.

He deleted it, then brought it back. The guy on top had a black body. The heads had been crudely pasted on. No webmaster did this. Still, it was more than Mandy could have done. A friend of hers? Someone else altogether?

He felt nauseous but popped a Vic anyway. Then he locked his bedroom door and dialed up Aunt Thumb, the Back Pack's favorite porn site, teen guys and older women. It always aroused him.

Nothing tonight. What's up? Not up. Too tired, stressed? Too gay?

He fell into a restless sleep. Driving Sarah's car with the No. 80 through the maze, the carwash brushes slapping against the windshield, up the stairs, with Romo howling, and right out a third floor window, trying to make the car fly. Fighting the stick shift, a little white bat, but the ground was coming up fast and the hard thump of the bass beat out of the CD player was pounding his skull. Pounding.

It was Junie pounding. Morning. He had left the bedroom door locked overnight. Time for school.

In the hallways, he could shut out the sound, but not

the look of laughter, the grinning, the eye rolling, the open mouths. Had they all gotten the e-mail from COACHRIGHT69? Did they all know about the picture in his locker? Even teachers were giving him those knowing half smiles, the big stud couldn't get it up for a horny slut. He felt like smashing their faces in. He couldn't wait for practice to start.

Tyrell tried to talk to him as they jogged out onto the field, but Matt brushed him off. Now he wants to talk to me. Forget about it. Enough little plucking fingers in my mind. Got to stay clear.

When he told Dorman he wanted to try a few plays at cornerback, the coach nearly peed in his pants. On the first play, he snatched a pass out of Heller's hands; on the second, he hit Pete so hard he coughed up the ball. Coach Mac ran over, whacking his clipboard, "Way to go! Way to go!"

Another great practice.

He avoided Tyrell, didn't shower after practice, and drove straight to the gym.

The ironheads razzed him about last week's game, but one of them came over to spot when he started lifting alone. As tired as he was, rage fueled him. On sheer will, he pressed three hundred pounds.

"Easy, man," said the ironhead, looking down at him. "You don't need to crush the football, just kiss it."

He almost dropped the bar before he realized the

153

ironhead had said "catch," not "kiss."

Am I going nuts?

Tyrell was waiting for him in the parking lot outside the gym, leaning against the Jeep's driver door. No way to avoid him now. But why didn't he come into the gym? Does he think I'm gay?

"Was it you?" said Tyrell.

"Fuck you, too," he said before his mind registered the words. "Was it me what?"

Tyrell's face was twisted. "I ever sell you weed?"

"What?"

"Listen to me." He seemed darker. "Did Tyrell Williams ever sell Matt Rydek marijuana?"

"What's going on?"

Tyrell screamed in his face, "Answer the fucking question!"

"No. You've like given me six hits, lifetime. Free. Why?"

Tyrell closed his eyes and leaned back against the Jeep. "Cops pull me out of class. Want to know if I'm dealing. Say the weed they found in that locker came from me. Say they have a witness, top stud on the team, like Captain America, ready to testify he bought weed from me."

Top stud? The one on top? He had to wrench his mind back to Tyrell. "You thought that was me?"

"Don't know what to think, man." Tyrell's eyeballs

were red. "Motherfuckers are squeezing me."

"Why?"

"Why you think? That thing gets out, you're gonna see the perfect shit storm. Everybody's fucked. So they find a way to tell Tyrell he better keep his mouth shut. You mean they haven't gotten to Captain America yet?"

TWENTY-THREE

He could visualize himself shutting down, an old trick he usually saved for games, but now he used it just to get through another day. Closing doors, shutting windows, pulling drapes across the glass. Look straight ahead. Narrow the ears, too. Grandpa used to turn off his hearing aid when he didn't want to hear any more of Grandma's babbling about the neighbors, the kids, the other members of the church choir.

If it's not about football, don't see it, don't hear it, don't touch it. Delete it. If it's not about football, it's spam. Smile and keep moving. He looked right through Sarah in the cafeteria. She stood frozen, eyes wide, mouth open.

He ripped through Friday's practice. They were supposed to be tapering off for Saturday's game against Southwood, sure to be a physical game against one of the toughest teams in the conference, but they were psyched, hitting hard, following Matt's lead. The coaches were afraid someone would get hurt, but they didn't want to turn off the energy. Chris didn't show up for practice again, although he dressed for the game and sat on the bench again. What's his game? Nobody talked to him.

Matt was so wired, he remembered the Southwood game only as a personal highlight reel. He'd never been in the zone so long and so completely. Might as well have been playing himself in a video game. Dad must have been screaming his lungs out. But Matt never heard him. Or anyone else in the crowd.

His seventy-yard touchdown run came on the third play of the game. Hunkies go long. His over-the-head one-handed catch in the end zone came toward the end of the second quarter. By that time they were up 21–3 and he was heading toward the school single-game yardage record. At the start of the second half, he persuaded Coach Mac to let him shift to cornerback on defense. He said he'd seen a way to beat their top wide receiver. He picked the ball out of his hands on the Nearmont forty-two and went all the way behind Ramp's big number 47. Ramp blocked like a tank. For a moment in the end zone, as they hugged, he felt something like love for Ramp, for what they had done together. Then he saw the smirk on the big face and clicked back into his icy focus.

The coaches gave Matt the game ball, and he trotted to the stands to give it to Junie, who hugged it like a baby.

Matt thought he should be feeling something after a game like that, but he was so calm inside, he felt hollow. While he was dressing, the froggy reporter came over.

"Great game, Matt. Were you like inspired today?"

"I had terrific blocking. And Brody put the ball right in my hands." Something Jerry Rice might have said after a game, he thought.

"It was like you had to prove something. You were playing out of your skull." The kid looked very serious. No dummy. Better be careful around him.

"I was in the zone."

The reporter brought his face close up under Matt's. "You know, like sometimes athletes play better when they're blocking out their personal lives."

What's he know? "What's the question?"

"Is what happened at camp still on everybody's mind?"

One of the managers came over. "Coach doesn't want you in here, Barry. You don't have athletic department credentials."

"We could do this by e-mail, Matt." As the manager started to push him out of the locker room, he handed Matt his card. "The *Nearmont Eye* is independent. Our motto is 'Uncensored news you can trust.'"

This time, Matt put the card in his pocket. Tricky sonuvabitch. Check out the *Nearmont Eye* sometime.

He popped Vics and slugged down beers that night as

158

he made the rounds of the parties. Pete volunteered to drive so he could celebrate. A junior girl he had danced with at the second party showed up at the fourth. They went upstairs. She was as drunk as he was. It was quick. No problem. I'm okay.

He slept into late Sunday afternoon. Dad woke him for dinner. When he said he wasn't hungry, Dad said, "A Rutgers coach is coming by for dessert and coffee."

"I don't want to go there." Way too close. You'd be on my case twenty-four/seven.

"Don't want you to. Might be leverage to sweeten a Big Ten deal."

When Junie took his dinner downstairs to the rec room to watch a CyberPup movie, Dad said, "What's with Tyrell?"

"What do you mean?" Tyrell had a good game, Matt remembered dimly, but hadn't showed up at any of the parties, which was not like him.

"Is he bringing dope from the city?"

"Who says that?"

"Cops talked to him. If he's busted, that's not good for us."

"Larry!" Mom shook her head. "What about good for him?"

"You need a strong runner to keep the secondary guessing so they can't key in on Matt," said Dad. "Too bad the Marin kid punked."

"The gay boy?" said Mom.

"He's not gay, not a punk," Matt blurted.

"He's running some kind of number," said Dad. "Claims he's sick."

"He got hurt."

Mom and Dad exchanged glances. What did they know? Mom said, "Vikki heard that his mother's angry at the world and wants Nearmont to pay for her pain."

"It's called blackmail," said Dad.

"What if he did get hurt?" said Matt.

"Suck it up—he's supposed to be a football player," said Dad. He looked at his wristwatch. "Rutgers coach here any minute. Jody, better if Junie stays downstairs."

"Why?" said Matt.

Dad's mask slipped on. "This is for you, Matt. Someday you'll understand."

"Understand what?"

"Recruiter sees Junie, might wonder about you."

"I'm not ashamed of him," said Matt.

"People don't think that way anymore, Larry," said Mom.

"Football coaches do. Let's get Matt into college, please?"

They ate silently until the doorbell rang.

The Rutgers assistant was a big, friendly young guy who asked for a second helping of Mom's pie and Dad's opinion on the Jets' secondary. He had them in his pocket by the time he turned his attention to Matt. "That was some game yesterday, Matt. So let me ask ya, the pass-play or the interception: which lit up your tree?"

Been there, pal. "Winning the game."

He hooted and slapped the table. "Why did I know you'd say that? Some boy you got there, Mr. Rydek. Rutgers is the perfect fit. We got the big three: geographics, academics, athletics."

Matt tuned out as the coach told them that Rutgers was near enough for friends and family to come out and root. A great university dedicated to a quality education. And the new head coach had been the receivers coach for the Dallas Cowboys, was into a passing game built around a classic quarterback throwing to big, fast wide receivers. The perfect place to showcase Matt if he decided to try for the NFL before—wink to Mom—law school or medical school.

He was winding down when he suddenly turned to Dad and said, "Heard good things about Rydek Catering."

"We've been lucky." Dad playing humble hero.

"You know, the athletic department gets a lot of alumni and corporate requests for catering referrals, especially now we've got the luxury boxes. That something you might be interested in?"

"Might be." Dad was trying not to sound eager.

"Give me a bunch of your business cards."

The coach was at the door shaking hands when Junie

and Romo clomped upstairs from the rec room. "Hi," said Junie.

"Hi. What's your name?"

"Lawrence Michael Rydek Jr., but you can call me Junie. And this is Romo. She was named for Bill Romanowski, Dad's favorite player."

Dad shot Mom a shut-him-up look, but the coach was laughing and clapping his hands. "That Romo looks like a smart, tough dog to me. Junie, soon's I get back to school, I'm gonna send you a Scarlet Knights T-shirt and cap, and a Rutgers dog collar for Romo. But you have to make me a promise."

"Sure." Junie was bouncing on his heels.

"When you come to Matt's games at Rutgers next year, you'll wear the cap."

"Awwww-right."

The coach waved and made his big exit. Division One performance, thought Matt.

"He's very nice." Mom laughed.

"Slick," said Dad. "I'd like to see a catering contract in writing."

TWENTY-FOUR

Tyrell always said that the week leading up to Homecoming was like a week back in the 'hood, all noise and action, no downtime. You had to shake with the beat or die from the heat. But this year's beat was slower, softer, and there was no heat. There was less buzz in the halls, Matt thought, fewer PA announcements for committee meetings, ticket sales, volunteers. Even the hammering and sawing on parade floats out on the front lawn seemed toned down.

Tyrell himself was a shadow, quiet in the halls and cafeteria, doing only enough in practice to keep the coaches off his tail. Pete was jittery. Even All-Brody, the calm cruiser, seemed super alert, like a dog sniffing strange smells. None of them had much to say to Matt, which made him feel even more alone. The Back Pack was drifting apart.

But Mandy was drifting back. It started with a look from the sidelines as he passed cheerleader practice. No expression he could read for sure, but she didn't turn her back. Brody spotted it, raised his eyebrows until Matt said, "What?"

"You could reel her back in if you wanted." The way Brody said it, super casual, made Matt think he was carrying a message. Just the way he brought Coach's instructions into the huddle, trying to make it sound like they were his ideas.

"Who says I wanted?"

"Terri says she wasn't so flamed at you pounding Sarah as she was losing out on Queen for nothing." Brody gave his I-could-care-less shrug.

That sounds like old Mandy, Matt thought. The unwritten rule at Nearmont was that the Homecoming Queen couldn't be going out with a football player. An ancient rule, nobody knew why it was obeyed, but Mandy had gone along, not even allowing herself to be nominated. She'd liked it when a friend of hers won and asked her to ride the float with her as a lady-in-waiting. Everyone would know she was the real queen. But now she just looked like a loser. No crown, no football player boyfriend.

"So?"

"Ask her to Homecoming—she'll suck your dick till your head caves in." Brody looked proud of himself. He repeated it. "Sound like a song?"

"I'll think about it."

"Clock's ticking, old buddy."

After practice, he found Junie waiting by his car. Damn. Wasn't I going to start him on a fitness program?

"Need a ride?" Junie usually rode home with one of the women who worked in the cafeteria.

"Yep. Guess why." He was grinning and clutching a long green plastic envelope.

"Mrs. Arecco was sick."

"Nope." He was bouncing on his feet. "Guess again."

"I give up."

"I'm taking music lessons." He opened the envelope and carefully pulled out a black plastic tube with holes and a mouthpiece. "It's called a recorder." He blew a note. "Daniel says I'll be playing songs in a month."

"Who's Daniel?"

"My friend Daniel is in the marching band. He's Sarah's friend, too."

Great. Now she's worming her way back into the picture.

He dropped Junie off at the house, promising to listen to him practice when he got back from the gym.

Monty waved him into his office and closed the door quickly. "What's going down?"

"What do you mean?"

"I'm asking you. The cops have been around, asking questions."

"About what?"

"Why do you guys always answer a question with a question?" Sounded like Monty had talked to other guys. Which ones? "What do you know? And don't say, 'About what?'"

Matt glanced at the metal locker where Monty kept the juice. Not too cool. Monty followed the glance and tilted his head in a questioning way. Matt wondered what he'd have to tell him to get his shot. Nothing. Not going to tell Monty anything.

He didn't have to. Monty said, "No, it wasn't about juice. They wanted to know about Tyrell—did he ever deal pot in here, which he didn't. And they asked me if Chris Marin ever worked out here. What's his story?"

"Marin looked good at camp, but he got sick and there's some kind of fuss." Close enough, no lie.

"Heard that." Monty opened the metal locker and took out the FedEx box. "Anything I need to know?"

"It's all I know."

Monty nodded and started laying out the needles and syringe. "Word to the wise, Matt: You keep your eyes on the prize. Another game like the last one, your dad'll be beating off coaches with a bat. Now, grab your ankles."

He needed to push the image of a bat into a corner of his mind before he could try to imagine the steroids coursing through his body, pumping and ripping muscle. But the fantasy wasn't working today. Hope the juice is.

After dinner, he sat in Junie's room listening to him blow on his recorder until Dad clomped upstairs. Mom was at a PTA meeting for Homecoming. "Man, I thought Romo was being tortured."

"He likes it," said Junie. Romo was staring up at Junie, tongue out, digging the sound. Matt hated it, a whiney note that picked at his brain like a red fingernail.

"Matt, I need to talk to you." Dad turned his back and started out of the room.

"When Junie's done." He threw the words like rocks at Dad's broad back.

As Dad turned slowly, Junie said, "I'm done." Good old sensitive Junie. I'm probably not ready for Armageddon tonight anyway, Matt thought. Just edgy. The 'roids? That's the least of it.

He followed Dad downstairs to his den. Big meeting? Lecture? Ultimatum? Cross-examination? Been there, bring it. But Dad pushed him down gently into his leather couch and sat next to him, a hand lightly on his arm.

"I think I've been on your back too much lately, Matt. For your own good, but still too much. You're a great kid, all I could have wanted, and I know you've got a lot on your plate this year." Dad's eyes looked soft, sincere. He was playing good dad. "Something on your mind?"

"Homecoming," said Matt. "Big game."

Dad nodded. "Team up for it?"

"Hope so."

"This thing with the Marin kid? Negative effect?" He was trying too hard to sound cool. What did he know?

"Coach thinks so." When Dad's eyes widened, Matt said, "Without him, it's easier to key on me and Tyrell."

The eyes narrowed. He looked disappointed. Then the expressionless mask came down. Bad dad's back. Fine. Familiar territory. "Something happened on Raider Pride Night. Can't help you if you don't tell me."

"Tell you what?"

Muscles twitched in the mask—he was trying not to show he was getting pissed. "Something that could affect the program, the school, not to mention everything we've worked for."

"What happened?" He looked Dad right in the eyes, challenged him. You think you know everything.

Dad didn't blink. "Something that needs to stay in the locker room. Stay with the team. What do you think?"

Maybe he does know. Maybe he's afraid it's going to get out, wreck the season, hurt the town, hurt Rydek Catering. "It was a Raider thing."

"That means it stays in the locker room, right?" When Matt nodded, Dad said, "Everybody on that page? Tyrell? Pete?"

"Why do you mention them?"

"You always wonder—a kid who doesn't really live in the town, another kid who always seemed a little . . . sensitive?"

"They're cool."

Dad clapped Matt on the shoulder. "Good boy." He pushed himself up out of the couch. "I got a pile of e-mails to answer. Would you believe Mississippi State?"

"Coach played for Bear Bryant." Saw that on ESPN.

"Right." Dad was moving toward his computer. "Trouble is, he loves running backs, not receivers."

Matt was relieved the meeting was over, and disappointed. Did he want a *Law & Order* third degree? I wanted something out of him, like he was interested in what had happened to Chris, maybe how I felt about it, not just how to keep it quiet so it wouldn't give the town a bad name. What the hell, I'd have lied to him anyway.

He heard Mom drive into the garage. He hurried into the kitchen, grabbed a can of soda and a leftover broiled chicken leg, and went up to his room. Junie was playing his recorder again. That one note made him happy. Even if Sarah did it only to get to me, it was a good thing.

He felt Jerry Rice watching him slam down chicken so fast he got a lump in his chest. Ease up, bro, you need to be steady, in control, if you want to snag the rock.

The glowing computer screen called him over. He played a few games of Bubblehead. Corndog said it was good for eye-hand. Got bored and checked the ball scores, read the rants on ESPN.com. Visited Aunt Thumb. Same old faces and bodies. Boring. He stalled as long as he could before he checked his e-mail.

Most of the messages were spam or from the Raiders coaches and managers. He deleted them. One from Paul@Nearmonteye. He deleted that. Didn't feel like answering questions. He was surprised to see one from CRAZYOVER80. He clicked on it.

> Dear Matt,
> Now I know what you meant when you once said you have to get past the past. This is no way to say good-bye. I want you and I need you. I love you.
> Amanda.

It didn't even sound like her, he thought. What does she sound like? I never listened to her. She never had anything to say. How would I know that if I never listened to her? Great, let's get deep here. I don't know who she is any more than she knows who I am.

He deleted it.

A message from SONOFAGREENBERET. Probably spam, but he clicked on it.

> Hi Captain Matt. Got to talk to you. Chris

He shut down the machine.

TWENTY-FIVE

On Wednesday, three days before Homecoming, Coach Mac called Matt and Ramp out of class. That was unusual. Matt figured it was about Chris. His stomach hurt. Coach was rocking in his swivel chair behind his big desk. He told them to close the door and to sit down. Matt sat on the edge of his chair. It was hard to see Coach behind all the trophies, videocassettes, and stacks of papers on his desk.

"What's going on, captains? No bullshit."

Ramp said, "Lotsa pressure, Coach. It's a must-win."

"I said no bullshit. What about Tyrell?"

"Somebody narced him," said Ramp. "We think it was Eastern Valley, psych warfare. I, personally, have never seen him dealing."

With Ramp's big, dumb potato face it was hard for people to pick up on what a tricky scumbag he was, thought Matt. First he spreads rumors about Tyrell, then he vouches for him.

"What do you think, Matt?"

"I know Tyrell's not dealing. But getting pulled in shook him up. Maybe you could talk to him. Like a vote of confidence."

Coach Mac nodded. "Anybody talk to Chris Marin? He's not in school."

I spent the night not talking to him, thought Matt, wondering if I should answer his e-mail. Didn't exactly wimp out. Just haven't done it yet.

"That homo is trouble," said Ramp.

"What makes you say that?" Coach Mac rocked forward. Matt thought his ears perked up, like Romo's.

"When he saw he didn't have the goods, he played the blame game." Incredibly, Ramp sounded as if he believed what he was saying. "Like we gave him a hard time."

"Did you?"

"Sure. Raiders pay their dues. We all did."

"Swirlies?"

"No. We tea-bagged him and he freaked. It happens to closet fags."

What do I say? thought Matt. Coach is buying this. And Ramp isn't totally lying. Yet. Chris did freak. Could he be gay?

"His mother hired a lawyer," said Coach Mac. "Claims he was sexually assaulted."

"By who?" said Ramp. What balls he has, Matt thought.

"She doesn't know and Chris isn't talking. But she says she has medical reports; the boy had bleeding consistent with anal penetration."

"Proves he's a fudge packer," said Ramp.

"I don't like that talk," said Coach Mac. "You know what could happen to the program if this gets out?"

"What gets out?" said Matt. Coach was sounding like Dad. Had they talked?

"These are very serious allegations. Could shut us down, end the season." He swept a big forearm across his desk, clearing room so they could see his big, stony face. "You're the captains. The players will listen to you. No more loose talk. Put a lid on this until we find out what really happened."

"You want us to ask around?" said Ramp. Matt could tell he was trying not to grin. "Investigate?"

"No, no," said Coach quickly. "This is not a witch hunt. We're not trying to hurt anyone, not the team, not this poor kid. You understand?" He stood up and came around his desk. "Let's just make sure we keep this in the locker room until we can sort it out." When Ramp stood up, they squared off, yelled "Raiders Rule!" and bumped fists.

Matt just nodded at the coach as he left the office. He couldn't bring himself to bump fists with him.

Outside, Ramp said, "Who you think we got to worry

about besides Pete?"

"Pete won't say anything."

"Pete pisses sitting down."

"Worry about Hagen and Boda."

"They don't scratch their asses without asking me. Anyway, they know it was self-defense, if it comes to that." Ramp grinned. "Long as Missy Chrissie keeps her mouth shut, we win Conference, maybe State. Should I talk to her?"

"Leave Chris alone."

"Maybe not. Maybe he really liked it."

"Stay the fuck away." Matt was surprised at how hard his voice had become. Probably can't take him, Matt thought, especially if the fight lasts more than a few minutes, just too much size and weight. But I could do a lot of damage. His gut is soft, and I might just get lucky.

Ramp must have thought the same thing, because he put up his hands. "Hey. We're on the same team. Don't you want to win?"

"Maybe not if it means fucking somebody up." Had he ever thought about that before?

"You know, a man does what it takes," said Ramp. "A captain makes sure every man can do what he needs to do when the shit hits."

"A captain takes care of his men." Where did that come from?

"Like you know what a captain does." Ramp's big face

was expressionless, a mask like Dad's, his eyes slits. "You took the job because it looks good when you're up for a D-One ride, pretty boy with the ball gets the publicity and the pussy." There was spittle in the corner of his mouth. "How far you think you'd get without the grunts blocking for you? I'm the one does the dirty work, keeps this team together. You don't like it, just stay out of the way."

He walked off.

When he gasped, Matt realized he had been holding his breath.

They avoided each other at practice, but Matt noticed they were both scanning the team, as if searching for someone who might tell about Raider Pride Night. Only take one loose mouth to start an investigation.

Do I want someone to talk? Pop the blister, take the pressure off so I don't have to keep all this inside?

Outside the field house, he smelled Mandy's lemony perfume before he felt her arm slip through his. She pushed her breast against him as if she expected him to feel it through his pads. The team jogged past them to the locker room. There were a few whistles.

"I was such a bitch," she whispered. "I thought you cared about that slut. Really hurt me. I wanted to hurt you. How could I have done it?"

"The e-mails? The picture in my locker?"

"Ramp gave it to me. He said he knew how to get to you. How could I listen to that pig?" He'd forgotten how great she looked, the waterfall of straight blond hair, almost platinum now, the eyes even bluer behind tinted contact lenses, the baby pink skin tight over sharp bones.

"But you want to get past the past." He figured she'd never hear the sarcasm, and he was right.

"I do. We both made mistakes. And after you did Kristen, I knew it was just fast food—you were lonely and horny without me."

Kristen was her name? Guess I knew at the time.

"Gotta shower."

"You do reek." She laughed through her nose. Never noticed that before. He thought of Sarah's tinkly laugh. "Let's go to Homecoming and stand this school on its ear. They'll talk about it for years. Then we can have our own homecoming. No one's at the beach house this weekend."

A couple of times he'd been at her parents' weekend house on the Jersey Shore, but never alone. It was on the water.

"Don't make me get down on my hands and knees." She smiled. "At least not here."

He knew he didn't trust her and he thought he probably didn't like her. But he wouldn't mind tapping that ass again, at night on the beach.

And maybe that would make life normal, at least roll it back to where it was before Raider Pride Night.

"I'll call you," he said. At the moment he said it, he even thought he might.

TWENTY-SIX

That night, sitting in his room, trying to read a chapter in the global economy textbook and keep an eye on the Yankee game, he heard the family phone ring through the one-note wail of Junie's recorder. Junie better be playing songs soon, or Dad would break that plastic pipe. The phone kept ringing. Mom and Dad were out—more Homecoming meetings. She was helping decorate, he was supplying some of the food.

Why isn't Junie or the answering machine picking up? The ringing stopped.

I hardly get any calls anymore. Duh. You keep the cell off, except when you think Junie might call for a pickup. You don't want any calls.

Junie was knocking on the door.

"It's open."

He held out the phone. "It's Sarah."

Matt whispered, "Tell her I'm not home."

"I can't lie to her," said Junie. Loud. "She's my friend."

Thanks. Matt took the phone. "Hi."

"I'm calling to invite you to Homecoming." Her words spilled out high and quick. "The chorus. Singing? We each get an extra free ticket."

He liked that she sounded nervous. "Thanks. I'm going with somebody."

"No problem. See you around." Sarah hung up. Not so cool.

Junie said, "What's up, CyberPup?"

"Gotta do homework." He handed Junie the phone. "Keep practicing."

Junie nodded and shuffled away.

Matt closed his door and stared at the computer screen. IMs were popping in. Coaches, managers, Ramp. Mandy. Chris again.

Let's just get through the next game, win it, be 3–0, maybe then we can figure it all out. Get past Eastern Valley, get our championship season underway. Game after that against Hudson Catholic is nonconference, a breather. A chance to think this through. Not now.

He deleted all the team messages without reading them, reminders and pep talks, Ramp calling the usual players-only meeting before Homecoming. He deleted Mandy's two messages. They would be little love notes, about as sincere as a song on an iPod. Probably copied off a song on an iPod. There was nothing real about Mandy. Used to like that because then I didn't really have to deal with her. Her going nuts over Sarah was the first real thing. Hurt her pride. He pushed Mandy and Sarah out of his mind, a mistake, because that left an opening and Chris came in again.

Better open it.

Please call right away. I need to talk to you.

Can you smell sweat and fear in an IM?

The kid is getting squeezed. You know about that, Matt. Only Chris doesn't have the balls to suck it up and get past it. He wants to talk about it, like a girl. Whine about how he feels. Get everybody involved in his problems.

Maybe you should be involved. You're a captain. Raiders supposed to be able to talk to you.

I'm not really a captain. Got the job so I wouldn't play baseball.

And he's not really a Raider. Barely on the team after missing practices and two games.

That's not all his fault. Some of that's your fault.

Kid's in trouble. Maybe you're the only one who can help.

Help him do what? He's in no shape to play right now, so he can't help the team. Does he just want to talk about it, or does he want someone to back up his story of what happened on Raider Pride Night? Wreck the team.

Maybe you could talk him out of telling what happened. That would help everybody. But doing that would be tricky. You'd almost have to admit something happened that you shouldn't talk about.

How would you handle that?

A man does what it takes.

What does that mean?

His head hurt.

Deal with it after Homecoming. Don't lose focus. Win the big game. Then go talk to him. Just a couple more days.

He deleted Chris.

TWENTY-SEVEN

Boda and Hagen blocked the locker room door, grinning as they waved off coaches, managers, and trainers. Players only. By the time Matt got inside, Ramp was already standing on a stool in the middle of the space between the lockers and showers they used for team meetings. Ramp's arms were folded across his black tank top, muscles flexed. He must have just lifted to get that pump. When he spotted Matt, he said, "You want to talk?"

"All yours." Matt edged toward the showers so he could watch the meeting from the side. See how the guys react. He noticed that Tyrell, Brody, and Pete were not standing together. We always stood together. What happened to the Back Pack?

He didn't see Chris.

Ramp pointed to the clock, and Boda slammed the door shut and locked it.

"Listen up, Raiders!" Ramp's voice ricocheted off the stone and metal. "It's nut cuttin' time. Now's when we find out if Raiders are going all the way."

"All the way," yelled Hagen.

"Let's hear it," yelled Ramp. "Where we going?"

"All the way," the team shouted back.

"Better than that."

"ALL THE WAY!"

"Fuckin-A, all the way. If we stay together, they can't stop us. Raiders Rule!" He held up his fists.

"Raiders Rule!" The players held up their fists. Matt didn't, and he noticed that Tyrell and Pete didn't. Brody held up his football.

"Better than that."

"RAIDERS RULE!"

Ramp waited until the echoes slipped to the floor like little pools of shower water. He lowered his voice so the guys in the back had to push forward to hear him. "Lotsa shit been going 'round. People trying to bring us down. Hurt the team. People who don't want the Raiders to go all the way. We gotta stay tight. Gotta think team." He scanned the faces in the crowd. He found Tyrell, nodded at him, then at Pete.

Matt watched Tyrell look down. Pete turned until he found Matt. Pete's face was twisted— he looked like he was in pain. He must have said something to somebody.

"What's it mean to think team? It means you don't

talk team business with anybody who isn't on the team. It means whatever happens inside the team stays inside the team. It means you can only trust a brother Raider, somebody on the team. Any questions?"

"I got a question." A familiar voice roared out of the shower room behind Matt. "You want it in the face or the gut?"

Chris walked out of the shower room, dressed in his uniform. Must have been hiding in there. He held a small gray revolver in both hands, out in front of him.

Players scattered out of his way, leaving a wide path to Ramp, who turned his head slightly but didn't move his body. "Well, it's Missy Chrissie."

"I'm going to kill you."

"Oh, I thought this was how you were gonna get back on the team." Ramp laughed through his nose.

"Told you I had a gun, remember?" Chris's voice rose. "Blow your fucking head off."

"You don't have the balls." Ramp's voice got deeper, stronger. Matt thought, Ramp has all the balls.

So quiet in the locker room, Matt could hear breathing, farting as guys let go out of fear.

"First in your gut, then in your face."

"You're all talk, faggot." Ramp stepped off the stool. He looked at Chris over his left shoulder, facing him sideways. Less of a target? "You couldn't make the team, you can't pull the trigger."

Ramp's pushing it, thought Matt. I hope he knows what he's doing. Maybe I hope he doesn't. Some part of me wants to see Chris blow Ramp's head off. No, I don't. It wouldn't stop there. Wreck the season. Is that all I care about?

So do something, Cap'n Matt.

Yeah, like call the kid back when he needed you. Like yesterday.

"Chris."

"Matt?" He glanced over.

"Let's talk about this," said Matt.

"Talk when he puts the gun down," said Ramp. "He could hurt somebody."

"Guess who?" Chris tried to laugh, but it sounded more like gargling. The roar was long gone. "I want to see you on your knees."

"That'll be the day," said Ramp in his John Wayne voice.

Chris yelled, "On your knees."

"Put it down," said Matt. He took a step toward Chris, who glanced at him but kept the gun aimed at Ramp. His hands were trembling.

"Maybe I'll put it down when Ramp's on his knees," said Chris.

The kid's losing it, Matt thought. Chris doesn't know what to do. He isn't going to kill anyone. Maybe I can talk that gun down.

"We'll listen to you, Chris," said Matt, "when you put the gun down."

"I changed my mind," said Ramp. "We're not listening to this faggot. Hey, Chrissie, what's your dad in jail for, little boys?"

"Shut up," screamed Chris.

"He probably likes it up the shit chute, too."

The gun was shaking now.

"That's it, Ramp, I'm gonna—"

"How many bullets you got?" said Ramp. "One for every Raider?"

"Shut up, Ramp," yelled Matt.

Ramp grinned and turned his body to face Chris. He raised his arms, flexed, and made fists. "How many of us you think you'll get before we shove that gun right up your ass?"

"I'm gonna kill you." Chris was crying.

"Kill yourself, you little faggot," boomed Ramp.

Chris cocked the hammer.

"Get it over with," yelled Ramp. "Suck the gun."

"Shut the fuck up," yelled Matt.

"Do it, fag."

Chris moaned and put the barrel of the gun in his mouth.

"No," yelled Matt.

The world turned white and silent. He was in the zone. One long step, a hop, and he was launched, flying toward Chris, his hands reaching for the gun as if it were a ball. He knocked the barrel out of Chris's mouth and tried to get a finger under the hammer before it came down.

The flash blinded him, the blast knocked him down.

He scrambled up. Chris was sprawled on the floor, legs twitching. Blood, bits of hair, everywhere.

Ramp swaggered over. "Dead?" Maybe he said that. Matt's ears were ringing.

He imagined smashing his fist into the potato head, but the zone was still up—he was thinking clearly. Break my hand on that face. Go for the gut.

Like Dad taught you. Plant your feet, turn on the left foot as you bring up the right hand. The power comes out of your legs and butt.

Ramp went down on his knees, puking. Matt felt sick to his stomach.

TWENTY-EIGHT

The cops talked to Matt and Ramp until their fathers showed up, then let them tell the story again. No one seemed to notice that Matt and Ramp never looked at each other.

"Kids are heroes," said Dad, clapping Matt and Ramp on their shoulders. Mr. Rampolski, shorter than Ramp but wider, nodded and mopped his bald head. He couldn't stop sweating. Dad was hyper. "Could have been a massacre, Columbine, worse. Football captains, says it all."

The police chief cleared his throat. "Still some more questions, Larry. We've got an investigation here."

"Seems pretty clear-cut to me."

They were in the principal's office and she kept walking in and out, talking on a cell phone and a walkie-talkie. Some kids had come back to school after hearing about the shooting. Matt could make out their heads in the twilight outside the principal's window.

"Chief?" The principal beckoned him to a corner of her office. Matt couldn't hear what they were saying, even when the principal relayed it to someone else over her phone. Finally they nodded at each other and the chief said to everyone, "Okay, that's it for now. Probably want to talk more tomorrow. Be better if you don't talk to the media."

"They'll be camping outside our houses," said Dad. "You know how they are." Matt could tell he wanted to be interviewed on TV.

"Doesn't mean you have to talk to them," said the chief. "I can have them moved."

Dad said, "Dr. Jaffe? What about Homecoming?"

The principal looked annoyed. "There will be school tomorrow, although the regular schedule will be suspended. I hardly think a dance is appropriate under the circumstances."

"I agree," said Dad. "I was referring to the game."

"The football game?" She raised an eyebrow. "Look, Mr. Rydek, this is a very—"

"Of course, we all feel that way, but this is a community issue." He was expressionless, as tough as she was. "The boys need to stay together after this trauma, to release. If they don't play, the terrorists win."

"Terrorists?" She was getting mad. "This was a troubled boy—"

"Whom the school should have identified and done something about."

"Tomorrow," said the chief. "We'll talk tomorrow. Get some rest." He started herding Matt, Ramp, and their dads out of the office. "C'mon, Larry. Everybody wants to do the right thing here."

There were TV cameras on the lawn in front of the school among the Homecoming floats. Cops were keeping them behind yellow police tape. He noticed Paul Barry, the kid from the *Nearmont Eye*, talking to one of the TV reporters. Do I still have his card?

Dad said, "*Eyewitness News* here."

"Chief said no interviews," said Mr. Rampolski.

"Chief doesn't have a kid wants to go Division One," said Dad.

"I'm not talking to them," said Matt. He headed for the parking lot. Ramp and his father were right behind him. Dad paused, then shrugged and followed them.

Ramp caught up with Matt. "Your dad's right. We should play." It was the first words they had spoken to each other since the shooting.

"I don't know." He was exhausted, the way he felt at the end of a rough losing game.

"Nobody asked about Raiders Pride Night," said Ramp. "Nobody wants to know."

Matt stopped and turned to face him.

Ramp grinned. "No hard feelings."

"For what?"

"That punch in the locker room. Now we're even."

Matt walked quickly away before he could hit Ramp again.

TWENTY-NINE

Reporters were waiting outside the house, but he opened the electronic door with the remote in his Jeep and drove straight into the garage. Mom's car was already inside. Let Dad park in the driveway and deal with the vultures.

Coming up the back stairs into the kitchen, he heard Junie wailing his one note. Mom turned from the stove to grab Matt, hugging so hard, the steady ache of his ribs flared into pain. The cream wasn't working anymore. Did he need Sarah to rub it on?

"The first reports . . ." Mom started crying. "It was so long before we knew you were all right." When she let him go, she gasped. "That's blood."

"Turned him over to see if he was breathing." He remembered Chris's eyes. They seemed peaceful. Did Chris think he was going to die, that it was all over?

"The radio said he'd live but the doctors wouldn't

know for a few days how much brain damage he suffered."

Dad stomped in, jacked. "They were on me like white on rice. Told them I couldn't talk, ongoing investigation." So he had gotten his face on TV. "We need to make a plan."

"About what?"

"Can't let this get spun, the media, Marin's lawyer, the antifootball crowd, make it seem like— Come back here!"

He was on the stairs before he realized he was moving. He slammed his door and locked it.

Make a plan?

He felt nauseous. He hadn't eaten since lunch. Headache, too. Ribs hurt. He dug out a Vic. Never let pain get ahead of you—slows healing. Monty said that; the trainers, too. He washed the pill down with some warm Captain Morgan from the flask. Tasted like Romo's piss. He'd tasted that once, by mistake.

Junie's one note needled into his brain. Matt played an old Bone Patrol CD. Always counted on that one to smother anything, but it wasn't working anymore.

If I had answered his call, his e-mail . . .

Clear your head, Matt. Focus.

On what?

Homecoming game?

Be nice to talk to somebody. Just kick it around the way the Back Pack does. What do we talk about? Girls, football, lifting programs, girls, music, movies. All-Brody would make a joke. Tyrell's been so quiet lately. Pete might talk, but can't be sure where his head's at. Matt felt sad. These are my best friends. Who else is there? Forget about Mom, Dad, Monty, Coach Dorman, Mandy. He dug through some pants until he found the *Nearmont Eye* business card. Paul Barry. Home phone, cell phone, beeper, and two e-mail addresses. He put it on his desk. Maybe sometime.

Sarah.

Of them all, she was the only one he might be able to talk to. She would listen, maybe even help him sort out the mess in his head. But could he trust her? Maybe she told someone about what happened that night in her apartment. Didn't happen. Her fag friend Daniel.

Get past the past.

That's all I ever do.

He needed to get out of the house. Be great to work out, but he didn't want to talk to Monty and the ironheads. They'd want a bloody play-by-play. A night run? He remembered that Bergen Central had a lighted track. It was more than a half hour away, but worth the trip if he could clear his head.

Getting out was easy. The wailing of Junie's recorder covered his footsteps. Mom was watching TV and Dad was yelling into the phone in his den, door closed. The TV cameras were gone, the street deserted as he backed out of the garage.

Quiet evening in the suburbs, people eating, watching

TV, cruising, walking dogs. Matt felt lonely, almost teary. Suck it up, stud. You're going to get out of here soon, away from all this shit. Away from Dad. Like it's all Dad. Still be football, and still be you, Matt.

The Bergen Central track was busy—some varsity athletes, mostly older joggers—but there was room for everyone and he felt better being in a flow with other people. He settled into an easy stride, enough to get the blood moving and open his lungs, not enough to rattle his ribs. He ran for almost an hour, winding down into a slow jog before he stretched on the grassy soccer field in the middle of the oval.

"You from Nearmont?"

Two boys and a girl, his age. He remembered he was wearing a Raiders T-shirt. And that Chris had gone to Bergen Central. How had he let that slip his mind? Or had it?

"Yeah."

"Were you there?" The kid looked serious, even sad. That made him feel better about talking to them. He nodded.

"Hey, it's you." The girl was pointing to him. "Your picture was on TV. Mike Ryder?"

"Matt Rydek."

"You were the one grabbed the gun from Chris."

He looked down, spread out his hands. One of the kids said, "You don't want to talk about it?"

"Did you know him?" asked Matt. "Why did he leave here?"

The kids looked at each other, and when one of the boys nodded, the girl said, "His dad went to jail for, like, stealing from his company? And some of the older kids gave him a hard time."

"That's it?"

"Well, it got really bad. Chris started fights—he had a real attitude some days. He got suspended after he broke a kid's jaw. His mother needed to sell the house anyway, so they moved. What's going to happen?"

Matt shrugged. "They're trying to decide about the Homecoming game."

"It was just on the radio," said the girl. "They're gonna play, but not at Nearmont. Some neutral site."

Matt wasn't surprised. He wondered if Dad had helped work out that deal.

"Football." One of the boys shook his head. "Wouldn't want to miss the big game."

"You guys must be soccer players." He liked them and said it in a way that made them laugh.

"Lacrosse. Good luck, Matt." They waved and started running their laps.

He got lost on the way home, taking an unfamiliar road even as he knew it was a mistake. So we'll play the game, pretend nothing happened, and everything's just fine and I go to Michigan and win the Heisman and get drafted by the Giants and play in the Super Bowl and always know that some kid got wrecked for the rest of his life and even got blamed for it and I just stood around with my thumb up my ass because all I ever think about is me. Can I live with that? Is that what a real man does?

I'll get my ticket out of town, but I'll still be me.

And Chris? He was in trouble and I didn't do anything. I was his captain. He thought I was his captain. He should have been able to depend on me. I can't even depend on me. So what if I say something and there's an investigation and the season's canceled and I don't get a major Division One scholarship and I end up at a no-name school close to home, Dad on my back? Is that better? Who does that help?

He drove fast on the dark road. The turns came up before he was ready for them. Sometimes he took them on two screaming wheels.

Big headlights blazed, a truck coming right at him, and he wondered what it would feel like to drive right into all that hot, dazzling light, the end of all pain, all the Vicodin in the world in one massive, final dose.

He thought of what Dad had said about guys who couldn't take the heat, who drove into a tree because they couldn't pay the price.

A horn blasted and he swerved.

He pulled off the road and waited until he stopped shaking. Then he slowly found his way home.

THIRTY

He was a hero, and it felt bitter and wrong. Kids honked and waved on the drive to school. It took him almost fifteen minutes to make his way from the Super Senior parking lot to the big front doors, usually a two-minute walk. Kids wanted to shake his hand, talk to him, touch him; one jerk actually wanted him to autograph his photo on the front page of the local paper. It was his football picture. He pushed past the kid. In the lobby, teachers and staff applauded when they saw him. Mandy ran over and threw her arms around his neck. Cameras flashed.

"You saved our lives." She whispered into his ear, "I love you, Matt."

He felt phony, dirty. He unpeeled her and trotted to homeroom.

There was a feeling of celebration in the halls. One

of us is lying in intensive care, half his head shot off, and we're all so happy. The story had blown into a Homecoming float of a story. Chris's little gray revolver had become an AK-47, and he planned to wipe out the school after he wasted the football team. Probably had bombs somewhere.

I could have stopped it, Matt thought. All I had to do was hit Reply on my computer. Call back.

There were assemblies and group counseling sessions. Be aware of other kids who might be troubled. Talk to somebody if you feel bad. Thanks. He hit the mute, coasted. Coach Dorman held his class and Matt sat in the rear with the Back Pack.

"Anybody?" Dorman looked around the room.

Patel raised his hand. "Those tests you were going to give us? Would that have picked up Marin's homicidal tendencies?"

"Great question, Jay. The NFL in particular has been using psychological evaluations to . . ."

Matt let it fade into a dull buzz. Homicidal tendencies. What bullshit. More like delayed self-defense.

Coach Dorman grabbed him on the way out. "You okay?"

"Yeah."

"You kept shaking your head while I was talking. Something you want to tell me?"

For a moment, he did. Dorman looked sincere. But he

was a coach. "Sorry, just brain farting."

"You have every right. But if you feel the need to talk, get it out. Your folks, Pastor Jim, a coach, you know I'm here for you twenty-four/seven. You went through something there, like combat or 9/11." He patted Matt's shoulder. "The greatest interception of your career. So far."

He mumbled something and left the classroom. I blew the interception, Coach.

The team didn't dress for practice because the police didn't want them in the locker room. It was still a crime scene. State and county cop cars were on the grass outside the field house, and cops patrolled the yellow tape. There were a couple of TV crews hanging around.

Matt noticed a Rydek van parked outside the back entrance to the cafeteria. Dad was at the meeting about the Homecoming game. He'd be handling the food at the neutral site. Would he be picking up Junie today? Matt switched his cell back on in case Junie called for a ride. He caught up with Brody and Pete. They had nothing to say to each other.

Coach Mac stood in the middle of the fifty-yard line and waited while the assistant coaches assembled the entire squad in a circle around him. The TV crews stood on chairs behind the squad and taped.

"Listen up, gentlemen. I'm going back into a meeting about tomorrow's game." He raised his hand to shut down the shouts. "But it's only a game. What you went through yesterday was what football prepares us for. Captains!"

He waited until Matt and Ramp were standing on either side of him. He took their hands and held them up. "What these men did yesterday made me feel that what I do is worthwhile. I know some of you roll your eyes when I talk about the meat grinder of training camp, about getting past the past. I know some of you shut off when I say, 'If you can be a Raider, you'll know you can be one helluva man.' Well, this was what I was talking about. In years to come, on Raider Pride Night, instead of reading that letter from number 75, they'll be telling the story of numbers 80 and 47 in the fight of their lives. Raiders Rule!"

The waves of sound slammed against them. "Raiders Rule! Raiders Rule! Raiders Rule!"

Coach Mac waited for the echoes to fade away. "Got to go back now. Are you ready to play?"

This time, the sound seemed to make the turf shake under them. Maybe I'm just feeling woozy, Matt thought. Coach Mac dropped their hands and marched through a path the team opened for him.

Corndog yelled, "Let's walk through some plays."

"You heard Coach," roared Ramp. "Let's do it."

"You believe this shit, Matt?" said Tyrell. "Motherfucker's just going to walk out of this."

"What should we do?" said Matt.

"I don't know."

Matt grabbed Tyrell's sleeve. "I'm serious, man. You got an idea?"

Tyrell shrugged loose. "You the captain."

I'm the captain.

Matt's phone rang. Ask Junie to wait for him, or come watch practice. "Wassup, CyberPup?"

"Matt?" It was Sarah. "In the cafeteria. It's Junie. Hurry."

He pushed through the team and sprinted to the cafeteria. There was a crowd in one corner. He elbowed people out of his way.

Junie was on the floor, on his back, screaming. His legs and arms were in the air, shaking. It had been a while since he'd had a fit. Sarah was kneeling beside him, trying to comfort him. Dad stood nearby in a half crouch, looking bewildered.

The recorder was on the floor, broken into two pieces.

Matt dropped to his knees, then got low enough to slip an arm under Junie's head and cradle it.

" 'S okay, Junie, Matt's here," he crooned, rocking him. "Everything's cool, CyberPup. Matt's here to take care of you."

Junie stopped screaming. After a few minutes, the shaking legs fell to the floor, trembled, relaxed. His eyelids fluttered. "Matt?" He slumped against Matt's arm.

Sarah held his hand and stroked his leg. "Daniel can get you another recorder."

"Don't want one." Junie was blubbering.

"Show's over," Dad barked. He began waving people away. "Let's go."

"Daniel said you were sounding good," said Sarah.

"He said that?" Junie sniffled.

"I thought so, too," said Matt. "It was louder. You were holding the note longer."

Sarah smiled. "Daniel said you were ready for a new note."

Junie smiled.

"You can take him home?" Dad was leaning over them.

"Sure."

"Meeting," said Dad. "About the game."

"The game," said Sarah. She waited until he left. "Anything else we should be doing?"

"He'll be okay now." Matt dropped his arm behind Junie's back and sat him up. "Ready to rock 'n' roll, CyberPup? Let's get you home."

Sarah helped him pull Junie to his feet. He wobbled for a few steps, then seemed to be getting steadier.

"I'm sorry," said Junie.

"Not your fault." They said it together, looked at each other, and almost laughed. Bit their tongues. Junie'd think they were laughing at him.

"I didn't mean to break it," said Junie.

Matt looked at Sarah. She said, "Your dad came out of

the meeting, he was arguing with the principal, and Junie was playing his note. He screamed at Junie to stop, and Junie got upset and twisted the recorder a little too hard."

Matt stroked Junie's head. "Sometimes I get so upset by Dad, I do something I don't want to do."

"Really?" He leaned against Matt all the way out to the Jeep. Sarah held Junie's hand.

They pushed Junie up into the passenger seat and faced each other.

She said, "Well, um, I . . ."

"Sarah? Can we go someplace and talk tonight?"

She clenched her brow. He wondered if she was hesitating. Had he read her wrong? But she was thinking. "Our place?" she said, and laughed. "That diner."

He almost bailed out, imagining they would go back to her apartment again and the same thing would happen again—wouldn't happen again—but as if she were reading his mind, she said with a sad shrug, "Mom's home tonight."

"Seven?" he said, and she said, "See you."

THIRTY-ONE

Matt was a few minutes early, but she was already there, at the same booth in the rear they had sat in last time. He was happy to see her. Felt it in his chest.

"Hi." Best he could do.

"You were so great with Junie." Her big eyes were shiny.

"Happened before."

"The way you went right to him. Other people would have looked around, yelled at your dad, said something, but you just did what you had to do."

"Football." It was the first time he had thought about the game that way. "You don't let anything distract you. Focus. You were pretty cool, calling me."

"If it was my father I wouldn't have been cool, would have wanted to slug him." Her anger surprised him.

"Wouldn't have helped Junie." He felt his face relax

into a smile. "But it's a thought. What about your father? You see him much?"

She shook her head. "When he split, he made it seem like it was our fault, that Mom and I drove him out. He's a lawyer and he'd been planning it for a long time, even before his big birthday party." She was crying. "He took everything, the bastard. I hate him."

He squeezed her hand. He felt like slugging her dad. "It's okay to hate them," he said.

Was he saying that for her or for himself? He thought of all the hours throwing a baseball or a football with Dad. Those were good times. He thought about Dad making him feel small, screaming from the stands. Bad times. Doing things he didn't want to do. He thought of the broken recorder. What was Chris's father like? What made him steal from his company? How'd Chris feel about that? Did he think his Dad did it for him? He thought about the shrink with the thick neck.

They were quiet until the waitress came over and took their orders. Burgers, fries, soda. Same as last time.

"Why is the Homecoming game so important to your dad?" said Sarah.

"There'll be major college scouts there. It's important I go Division One so I have a pro shot."

"Important to him or you?"

That stopped him. He wanted to give her an honest answer. "I'm not sure anymore." The answer rattled something loose inside him, something scary. But good scary, like before a game.

Not sure? How could he not be sure if football was important to him, too?

"You still here?" She was smiling at him.

"Sorry." He blurted what bubbled up into his mind. "Sometimes I feel like I'm trapped in football." He stopped. "Let's talk about something else."

She nodded. "How's Junie?"

"He's okay. He gets overstressed sometimes."

"Daniel's getting him a new recorder."

"Your chorus fag friend." That came out before he could swallow it back.

"That's not like you." Her eyes got hot.

"You told him, didn't you? About us. What happened. What didn't happen." He was amazed to hear himself. It was that scary loose thing in his chest.

"I wanted to. I thought something was wrong with me." The words rushed out of her. "I really felt like I failed, and you would compare me with Mandy and all your other girls and I'd never see you again. But I didn't tell him." She reached across the table and grabbed his hands. He let her hold them down. "I—I really care about you, Matt."

"You really cared about getting into the hot crowd, beating Mandy. That's why you came after me." Where was this coming from? he wondered. Why am I testing her like this?

Her cheeks got red. "That's a lot of—" She took a breath. "In the beginning, yeah, I guess so. "

"Now?"

"Now it's about you."

"What if I wasn't captain of the football team, what if I wasn't even on the team?"

"I hate football." She made a face. "Loud, know-it-all bullies. Have to dominate everything. Raiders Rule. Rule what?"

He wondered if he had said too much to her, and he wondered how much more he could tell her.

He said, "Will you come with me right now?"

THIRTY-TWO

There was a police officer outside Chris's hospital door, but he recognized Matt and went inside to get Chris's mother. She came right out, a big, dark-haired woman who threw her arms around Matt. "Chris always talked about you. Thank you for saving his life."

"How is he?"

"They've got him heavily sedated until the swelling goes down, but he'll be all right." She looked over his shoulder.

"This is Sarah. My . . . friend."

Mrs. Marin took Sarah's outstretched hand and pulled her close. "So nice you came. Nobody's been here except the police."

"Chris talked to them?" Matt couldn't tell whether or not he wanted to hear that Chris had told them about Raider Pride Night.

"No. Be days before they bring him out of it." She started to cry. "He's under arrest."

Sarah put her arms around Mrs. Marin and held her until she stopped shaking.

"Can I see him?" said Matt.

Mrs. Marin nodded, but the cop at the door hesitated about letting him in. "I'm not supposed to, Matt, so be quick and don't tell anybody."

The turban of bandages around Chris's head and the spaghetti of tubes and wires attached to his body didn't surprise Matt as much as the expression on his face. He looked relaxed, almost happy. Maybe that was it. Nothing to worry about. Other people were doing all the worrying for him now.

Matt found a bare place on Chris's arm, between a tube in the crook of his elbow and a tube in his wrist. He gripped his arm there.

"Hey, Chris, it's Matt. Your captain." He stared at Chris's pale face, willed him to give a sign that he heard. Just flutter your eyelids, man. Nothing. The monitors hummed. "Hang in there, buddy. When you get through this, I'll be there for you. Promise."

Outside the room, Mrs. Marin hugged him again. He expected her to ask about training camp, but she didn't. He wondered what he would have told her. He said he'd come back soon.

In the hospital parking lot, Sarah said, "Nobody else

came to visit him? Coaches, players?"

"They want Chris to die."

"Matt, that's terrible, people aren't—"

"I'm telling you."

She winced at the harshness in his voice. "Why? He didn't end up hurting anybody except himself."

"They hurt him first. We all did." He felt nauseous. Wasn't the Vics, because he hadn't taken any since Dorman's class, six, seven hours ago. Wanted to be sharp. Maybe I need to cut back that shit.

"Raider Pride Night?" she said.

"You know?"

"There were rumors that something happened. There was something in the *Nearmont Eye* . . ."

"I let it happen."

"But you didn't do anything bad, did you?"

"Same thing."

"No, it isn't. Not if you do something about it."

"Like what?" He knew the answer. "It could wreck the program. People get arrested. No more games. No Division One scholarships."

"What happened to Chris that night?"

"It was really bad." He forced himself to delete the picture that popped up behind his eyes: Chris on his knees, shaking, the bat sticking out of him.

"Do the coaches know?"

"They want to believe he just couldn't cut it, be a Raider."

"You should try to tell them the truth. Then it's their problem, not yours. You did something."

He thought of Dorman. Be easier to talk to him than to Coach Mac. He was a guidance counselor. He looked at his watch. Almost nine o'clock. Probably still in the football office. Worth a shot.

Sarah refused to go home. She said she would trail him to school and wait in her car. He argued with her, but not too hard.

THIRTY-THREE

The back door of the field house was open. Corndog was in his office and never looked up as Matt tiptoed past. Dorman was alone in the meeting room, projecting Eastern Valley's offensive formations out of his laptop onto a wall screen.

"Can I talk to you?"

"Matt! Sure." He pointed to a chair, but when Matt kept standing, he said, "What's up?"

"Went to the hospital. Chris is under arrest."

"Attempted murder."

"He had reasons."

"Don't we all. Want an energy drink?" He reached into a cooler.

"Something bad happened to him on Raider Pride Night."

"That's no excuse to—"

"Really bad. Like . . . getting a plastic bat shoved up his ass."

Dorman didn't flinch. "Sounds like a ritual got out of hand."

"More like a rape." The word startled him. Of course, that's what it was.

Dorman took a deep breath, put down the bottle, and stood up. "Serious charge. Who else knows about it?"

"All the seniors. The freshmen were there, but they were blindfolded."

"So they didn't see it?"

"They know something . . . got out of hand."

Dorman didn't react to the edge in Matt's voice. "So that's why he came to kill you all."

"I don't think he came to kill anybody. I think he just wanted to make Ramp crawl, beg for mercy in front of the team."

"Not Ramp." Dorman shook his head. In admiration, Matt thought. "You talk to anybody outside the team?"

Matt shook his head. A lie, but he didn't want to get Sarah involved.

"I'm glad you came to me, Matt. Now we have to figure out the next step."

"The principal, the police?"

"Maybe. Although since no charges have been filed, except against Marin, it may not be necessary." Dorman frowned. "It's like preparing for a busted play. You have to think through the possible further damage. I'll try to get hold of Coach Mac tonight. We can all meet at school tomorrow morning, before we leave for the game. You talk to your dad about this?"

"No."

"I know he'd want you to keep it a Raider thing. Stays in the locker room for now. Go get some rest. Big day tomorrow." He put his hands on Matt's arms and steered him to the door. "You did the right thing, coming to me. Now get some rest and put everything out of your mind except the game."

Sarah was standing by her car. The 80 was still on her door. "So?"

"He's going to tell Coach Mac. We'll meet at school tomorrow."

"With the principal? The police?"

"That's what I asked. He said he wants to think through the possible further damage. Like a football game."

"He said that? Did he seem surprised?"

"Not really."

"So he knew."

As soon as she said it, he knew she was right. Why hadn't I picked up on that? Didn't want to.

"He mention your father?"

"Yeah. Said he knew Dad would want me to keep it in the team."

"Those bastards! Always taking care of themselves. What are we going to do now?"

She was making it her problem, too. He felt good about that.

"Here's what *we* are going to do. You're going home. I'm going to lift."

"What?"

"Work out, clear my head."

"Don't you want to talk to somebody? What about Pastor Jim?"

"Yeah, right. He thinks Jesus would be a linebacker like Ramp."

"How about a reporter?" said Sarah. "Get it out in the open—then they'd have to deal with it. Daniel has a friend on the *Nearmont Eye*, Paul Barry, he's a really good reporter and he could—"

"Later."

"Call me when you get home? Promise?"

"Promise." He wasn't sure who started the kiss.

"Poor baby. You had to hold it all in. It's not your fault."

"Some of it is. And I'm going to do something about it."

THIRTY-FOUR

The hot young moms were long gone and the yuppies were on their way out. The ironheads were there, strutting and screaming, banging metal. When they saw Matt, they nodded at him, raised their thumbs. But they were too cool to come over and ask him about the shooting. They'd do that later, he figured, making it part of something else.

For the first time, he felt sorry for them, then for himself. He could end up one of them, no college scholarship, working for Rydek Catering, pumping and popping pills.

He lifted until he lost track of his reps. Squats, curls, presses, flys melting into a ton of metal tearing at his muscles, squeezing the air out of his lungs.

"Easy, Matt." It was Monty. He handed Matt a bottle of water. "On the house."

"Thanks." He sat up, chugged the water.

"You want to lift to get bigger," said Monty, "not to destroy yourself. You don't want to get hurt, blow the season." He sat down on a bench. "I talked to your dad. He did a helluva job pushing the school board to let the game go on. You boys have worked hard, made sacrifices."

He thought of Chris, saw the bandage turban, the tubes. That's a sacrifice.

"Colleges getting real serious this time of year," said Monty. "Heard a scouting combine's coming out from the city to shoot the game with three digital cameras, then burn CDs for any coach interested."

Matt nodded. Why didn't he care?

Monty leaned closer. "Until this thing blows over, we're gonna keep the medicine cabinet shut."

"No shots?" Another way to squeeze me, Matt thought. It would have panicked him once; now he just heard it as noise from a distance. Am I just getting more numb, or is something changing? Maybe I don't need so much juice.

"You never know—reporters start fishing for one thing, come up with another. You'll be okay for a couple weeks if you taper off on the weight a little. I'll make up a new schedule for you." Monty stood up. "The heavy guys like Ramp, they've got the problem. They need a lot more gear than you do."

"Side effects when you stop?"

"You might feel a little down; that's normal. Let me

217

know—we'll find something for that." Monty slapped his arm. "You better go home, talk to your dad. He called about an hour ago to see if you were here. He's worried about you."

"Thought I'd steam first."

"If you're the last one out, just slip the lock on the front door. Leave the lights on. Cleaners come in tonight." He patted Matt's shoulder. "You're a good kid. I know you'll do the right thing."

"About what?"

Monty just winked.

On their way out, the ironheads drifted over, super casual. One of them said, "Wanna come have a drink with us? At Gus's, on 502?"

Would have been an honor once. "Thanks. I'll see you over there." A lie, but it got rid of them without more talk.

He showered and stretched out on a wooden bench in the steam room. He rarely steamed—it was boring and it took too much out of him. But he wanted to drift into that wet, weightless place without deadening his mind with Vics and alcohol. *I've been doing that for too long, deadening my mind. Got to be clear to figure out what I'm going to do.*

What am I going to do? The right thing? What's that? Let Chris take the rap for all this? He might be brain damaged anyway, no matter what his mother says, so what would it matter? Besides, what can they do to him that he hasn't done to himself already?

But why should Ramp get away with it? And make me part of it?

But if Ramp goes down, all the Raiders are screwed. No season. A trial, maybe jail. What college would touch us?

The steam room timer buzzed. He didn't remember setting it, but he'd been in long enough. He felt soft, loose.

The air outside the steam room hit his naked body with a cool slap.

"Cap'n Matt, in the flesh."

Ramp stood in the middle of the narrow passageway that led to the locker room, arms folded across his chest. Boda and Hagen were behind him. Matt wrapped his towel around his waist.

"Come to lift?" Matt tried to sound casual.

"Come to talk. What are you going to do?"

"Get dressed. Go home."

"You went to the hospital. You talked to Dorman. Something you want to tell me?"

"Yeah. You're in my way."

Ramp didn't move. "We're all in this together."

"In what?" The softness and looseness were gone. He noticed Ramp was wearing his tan work boots with his shorts and Raider tank top. His queer-crusher boots. Who was he planning to crush tonight?

"We gotta stick together, Matt. Keep it a Raider thing."

"Ramming a bat up a kid's ass is no Raider thing."

"We'll all go down for that."

"He might have died."

"I didn't shoot him." Ramp had no expression. Dead eyes. "You can't wreck the program over this little faggot."

"You gonna fuck me up, too?"

"Only if I have to. If you say you can get past this, be part of the team again, I believe you."

"I'll think about it."

"Not good enough. Got to know now."

He wondered how far Ramp would go to shut him down. He was scared, but he could manage his fear, use it for energy. "You sent those e-mail pictures."

Ramp grinned. "Pasting those heads on was a bitch. Should have paid more attention in Comp. Sci."

"The lies about Tyrell, about Pete."

"Linebackers blitz. I play hard, pal. So how about it?" Ramp stuck out his hand.

"You scratch eighty on Sarah's car?"

"Nice touch, don't you think? So can we close the chapter, get past the past?"

"I don't think so," said Matt. "You're in my way."

Ramp closed his hand into a fist. "With or without you, Matt, we're going for Conference, going for State. Raiders Rule!"

"Raiders Rule," said Tyrell from the darkness of the locker room.

Ramp whirled. Matt followed the angle of his head. Tyrell was gliding up behind Boda and Hagen.

"You don't want to be in this," said Ramp.

"I do," said Brody.

"Me, too," said Pete.

There were figures coming up behind them. Heller, Conklin, Patel. Matt's knees quivered; he could hear his heart beat, feel it fill his chest. He wanted to reach out, hug them all.

"You guys crazy?" said Ramp. "He's going to put us all in the toilet."

"Tyrell says we're already in the toilet. Tyrell just don't want to get flushed."

"Matt shoots off his mouth, you're flushed," said Ramp.

"Not how it works," said Tyrell. "Back Pack sticks together, tells the truth, we're gonna pay some price but we're not going down with you."

"Your people know about cutting deals," sneered Ramp.

"Your people made sure of that." Tyrell took a long step toward Ramp, who raised his fists.

"Hold it," said Matt. "I'm gonna meet Dorman and Coach Mac in the morning. See what they say."

"They'll say keep it in the family," said Ramp. "Who

do you think called me tonight?"

"What about the school, the police?" said Pete.

"Be he said, she said," said Ramp. "The principal and the chief don't want their town to look bad."

"I got to get dressed," said Matt. He took a step forward, but Ramp didn't move.

A football flew out of the darkness. Instinctively, Matt raised his hands and caught it.

"Get dressed, Matt," said Brody. "We got your back."

Ramp glanced over his shoulder. Patel, rapping a metal bar on the floor, was leading Heller and Conklin. They held bars, too.

"This ain't some sick-ass kid gonna eat a gun for you," said Tyrell. "We're Raiders."

"You're dead meat," said Ramp. "This ain't over." But he stepped aside to let Matt pass.

By the time Matt was dressed, the linemen were gone. Heller and Conklin were bumping chests, and Patel was toweling sweat off his face and grinning as if he had just kicked the winning extra point again.

Tyrell shook his head at them. "Potatohead's right. Ain't over."

Outside, in the parking lot, Matt said, "How'd you know I was here?"

"Pete called us," said Brody.

"Sarah called Lisa," said Pete, grinning sheepishly.

"Now what?" said Brody.

"Coach Mac, Dr. Jaffe, the chief, one of them'll do something," said Matt.

"Only if they got to," said Tyrell. "Look how Dorman sent Ramp after you."

"If the story's out, they're gonna have to deal with it," said Matt.

"Fuck us up," said Brody.

"Not as bad as this," said Matt. "Ramp's got us all by the balls now—we're all covering his ass, we're all his bitches. Get the truth out, we can deal with it."

"We're the Back Pack," said Pete.

"Back Pack plus three," said Brody, flipping the ball to Patel. "The Magnificent Seven."

They fell into a huddle, hugging, banging fists and shoulders, bitch slapping until the tension drained away and they began to laugh and sniffle with relief.

"Thanks, guys," said Matt. "I love you guys."

"You got a plan, Cap'n Matt?" said Tyrell.

"I do," said Matt.

I think I do, he thought.

THIRTY-FIVE

Dad was waiting in the doorway. It was almost midnight.

"You okay?" But it sounded more like Where-you-been? or What-the-hell's-going-on? than caring about him.

"Worked out."

Mom was right behind him. "Everybody's been calling, worried about you. Coach Mac, Pastor Jim—"

"Jody!" He shut her up. "Matt. We need to talk and we need to talk right now."

"About what?"

"Don't start that crap with me now." He reached out for Matt, nearly fell as Matt juked past him into the house.

Junie and Romo came clattering down the stairs. "Matteeeeee."

"Back to bed," snapped Dad.

"Have you eaten, Matt?" asked Mom.

"Not now," said Dad. "Matt, get your ass in the den."

Matt turned his back and started for the stairs. "Matt?" He could almost hear the gears shift in Dad's voice. "Please. We really need to talk."

The pleading in Dad's voice stopped him. The weasel will try anything. Might as well get it over with before this goes too far. Why put Mom and Junie through this, risk another fit?

He turned and walked into the den. Dad followed him, closed the door, and pointed to the couch. Matt sat in a hard wooden chair. Dad sat on the couch.

"Is it true?" Did he know or was he fishing?

"What?"

"No games, Matt. You know what I'm talking about." The gears had shifted again. The pleading was gone from his voice. "Something happened on Raider Pride Night that could ruin everything we've worked for all your life."

So he knew. Everybody knows. "You want to pretend nothing happened."

"I want what's best for you. What else do you think matters to me?" His eyes were filled with tears. Why don't I feel anything? thought Matt. "I love you, Matt. You are all I—" He stopped. "I don't want to see you end up like Freddy Heinz. Or me."

"It's not going to go away."

"It will if you keep your mouth shut."

"No chance."

"Get tough." Dad stood up. "Shit happens."

Matt stared at him.

Dad shouted, "Be a Raider!"

"I am a Raider." Matt stood up. "I'm not your Raider."

He held the stare. They were facing each other, about four feet apart. One step forward, Matt thought, and I will be in perfect range to knock him on his ass. And I can. I know he's thinking the same thing and wondering if I would. I've got two inches on him. He's got twenty pounds on me, but it's not muscle. Dad was staring back at him, as if he were searching for some sign of weakness. If he saw it, he would grab for Matt.

Dad didn't move. "What are you going to do?"

He stalled. "I haven't decided."

"It's not just your decision. There's the team, the town, your family. Affects everybody. College scholarships, business, property values."

"What about Chris?"

"Doctors said he'll be okay."

"Not if it comes out all his fault."

"Why should you suffer?"

"Because I didn't do anything when I could have. I was a captain. I should have stopped it."

"Okay. But you got to get past that now," said Dad. "Keep your eye on the prize."

"That's your prize, not mine."

"You ungrateful little sonuvabitch." His face was

226

hard, couldn't see his eyes. "Everything I did was for you, busting my back so you could have everything you ever needed, best equipment, baseball and football camps, money in your account, you know how much safe steroids cost. I'm not going to let you throw it away."

"You did it for you." Matt felt calm. In the zone. I'm the captain, he thought. My captain. "It's not your call."

He tried to step around Dad, but Dad grabbed his shoulders and pushed him back against the wall. "My house, my call."

Matt let his knees sag, pivoted on his left foot to turn right, just the way Dad had taught him, and cocked his right fist up at Dad's gut. No. Don't need to do that. He brought his left forearm up hard under Dad's chin, as if he were a tackler. As Dad stumbled backward, Matt banged the heel of his right hand against Dad's chest. It was just enough to put him down on his ass. Dad stared up from the floor.

"It's my call," said Matt.

Dad didn't say a word as Matt walked out of the den.

Mom was hovering in the hall. "Are you okay?" She sounded like she meant it.

He kissed her. "See you in the morning." He didn't want to talk to her now, lose what was in his head.

Junie was still awake, sitting on his bed clutching Romo. "Give me fifteen minutes on your wristwatch, CyberPup, then you and your killer dog come in my room. I got to do something first, and then we can start your training."

"Awww-riight. What's that?"

"Gotta get you in shape for the season. Bunches of crunches to start."

In his room, he winked at Jerry Rice. Catch you later, Number 80. I may be playing the outfield somewhere this spring.

He found the froggy online reporter's card on the desk. Let him get the story out. Coach, principal, chief, they're not going to be able to keep a lid on this. After it's in the *Nearmont Eye*, it'll be in the local paper, then on the TV news. Everybody's going to have to deal with what really happened, do the right thing. Whatever that is.

Gonna be a shit storm, Cap'n Matt.

You can deal with it.

Without juice and Vics and alcohol?

Need to stay sharp.

Man does what it takes. The loose, scary thing filled his chest. Bring it, I can take it. He flicked on his computer.

A man does what it takes.

While the machine connected to the Internet, he dialed Sarah's number.

Acknowledgements

In my long career as a sportswriter, I've been fascinated to watch how the values, both good and bad, of America's elite athletes have also become everyday values in our national life. From the schoolhouse to the White House, you can see loyalty and selfishness, bravery and bullying, working hard and winning ugly as easily as you can see it on the ball field.

But until I met Mike Miletic, I was watching what I call Jock Culture from the outside. He took me inside the mind of the athlete.

Michael J. Miletic, M.D., was my coach and partner in the creation and building of this book. While I did the actual writing, Mike's experience as a world-class athlete and sports psychiatrist is part of every page.

Let me tell you about him.

Mike was raised in Canada, a standout football and hockey player until he began weight lifting for extra strength and found out he loved pumping iron even more than pounding opponents.

Eventually, at 6 feet 2 inches and 242 pounds, he became a member of the Canadian Olympic weight-lifting team. The same week in 1982 he won a national lifting title, he was graduated from medical school. Injury ended his career before he could compete in the 1984 Games.

Mike's insight into the athletic mind has made him one of America's foremost sports psychiatrists. His Detroit-area practice includes professional, college, and high school players. He understands the joy of competition and he knows the dark corners of the locker room.

While the characters and events in *Raiders Night* are totally fictional—they are not drawn from Mike's files or my sports writing—they are not unlike characters and events that Mike and I have seen as doctor and reporter.

We think some of you may know similar characters in your lives and may even have been involved in similar experiences.

If you would like to write to us, we would certainly like to hear from you.

I can be reached at www.robertlipsyte.com.

Mike is waiting for you at www.mikemileticmd.com.